Munchkin's Tale of The Lollipop Club

Michael T Ernst

Published by Michael T Ernst, 2024.

MUNCHKIN'S TALE OF THE LOLLIPOP CLUB

First edition. October 1, 2024.

Copyright © 2024 Michael T Ernst.

ISBN: 978-1736401521

Written by Michael T Ernst.

To Jerry Marin, may he rest in peace.

MUNCHKINS LOLLIPOP Club, LLC
667 Holly Hill Drive
Casselberry, Florida 32707

PUBLISHERS NOTE: THIS is a work of fiction. Names, characters, places, and incidents are a product of the author's imagination. Locales and public names are sometimes used for atmospheric purposes. Any resemblance to actual people, living or dead, or to businesses, companies, events, institutions, or locales is completely coincidental.

BOOK DESIGN © 2020 BookdesignTemplates.com

Ordering information: Special discounts are available on quantity purchases by corporations, associations, and others. For details, contact the Publisher listed at the address above.

ISBN # 978-1-736-4015-2-1

ABOUT THE AUTHOR

I, Michael Ernst was born in Levittown, PA. I was raised with a loving mother and father, two sisters and a brother. Growing up in PA until the 9th grade. At this time my parents decided to move to Orlando, FL, and I graduated from high school.

My jobs over the years included pet sitter, paper boy, valet parker, warehouse worker, welder assistant, and a few more along the way. I also have a way of thinking outside the box and when my father retired, he asked me if we could start a business together. It took us a while before we both could agree on the same thing, and our new business was a billiard hall.

At this time in my life, I found my true calling of becoming an "inventor". During our time running a billiard hall I came up with a new idea for a billiard table, and billiard style board game which are patented.

The next year I went to the NY Toy Fair to get feedback on my idea and met with Marx Toy Company. They loved the idea of the billiard table and board game and signed a contract. The second day while walking around looking at displays a small lady came up from behind me and pulled my shirt. Upon turning around, she asked me, would like to meet the Lollipop Kid from The Wizard of Oz? She introduced herself as Elizabeth Maren, and walked me over to meet her husband, Jerry Maren. We both instantly hit it off and spent the next few hours discussing his days as a munchkin and mine as a toy inventor. I asked him one question. "Why was there never a munchkin movie?" He looked up at me and smiled. He said, no one has ever come up with an idea like that before. This bothered me and thought about it for a minute. At this point, I mentioned to Jerry if I would design a munchkin board game, would he support the idea. Again, he smiled and said, absolutely. We both agreed to meet the following year at the same place and would show him my design. A year later, we both met again in NY. I showed him the board game design, but I also showed him a story that I wrote while developing the board game. This is how I became the author of two books. The Untold Story from Lollipop Kid to Munchkin King, and The Munchkin Tale of the Lollipop Club.

MICHAEL T ERNST

MUNCHKIN'S TALES OF THE LOLLIPOP CLUB

CHAPTER 1

King Jerry's First Adventure

KING JERRY WALKED BACK over to his chair and asked Glinda, the Good Witch if she would sit next to him during the story.

Glinda happily said "Yes," as she walked towards him.

The King began to speak.

The tale I am about to tell has many parts to it. I can only speak of my part and that of my two best friends, Sammy, and Ray-Ray. What I have seen and heard. Other parts of this tale needs the help of the Good Witch, as she was also their mistress that knows some parts of both the evil Witches of the East and the West and part of the Good Witch of the South.

The king looked at Glinda and took her hand, she smiled at him and gave him a wink and he returned the wink.

The Good Witch looked at the king and answered, "yes, my dear King, I will tell the part of the tale when the time in your story calls for it. "

The King smiled at her and said, "Thank you." Let everyone here get seated and comfortable. All the town folks sat down on the lawn so they could see King Jerry and hear his words. Once everyone was seated, King Jerry took a drink from a cup and cleared his throat.

The story that I am about to tell happened when I was just a young boy. Let me tell you things were tough back then. We always lived in fear because of two evil witches, the Evil Witch of the East and West. They enslaved all the Munchkins and forced us to work their fields of banana trees and walnut trees, this was food that fed both Evil Witches armies of flying monkeys. The Witch of the East castle was a short distance from the border land between the lands of Good and Evil. The water that flowed through our town started in her land and if we did not pick the bananas and walnuts when they came into season, she would block our water supply. The Good Witch of the South and her sister the Good Witch of the North here today, did their best to defend us, but could not cross over to the land of Evil or they could be destroyed leaving us no protection of the land of Good. My two best friends at that time were Sammy, he was the oldest by a few days and Ray-Ray who was the youngest of the three of us; I was the middle aged one. Now, I recall my first adventure started around my twelfth birthday in the fall, the leaves were changing colors on the trees, and it was close to Halloween time, the favorite time of the year for Evil Witches! I was sleeping in my bed when I heard a tap on my bedroom window. I opened my eyes and saw Sammy and Ray-Ray looking in with their faces pressed against the glass window.

"Hey Jerry, are you going to sleep all day?" Sammy inquired.

I made my way to the window, "Hey, what are you guys doing here so early?"

"Did you forget what day it is?" Ray-Ray asked him.

"Quiet down, you guys are going to wake up my folks, go around to the front door; I'll be out in a few minutes after I get my backpack." I said to them. The boys gave me thumbs up and walked around my house to the front door and waited until it opened, and I stepped out carrying my backpack. I slowly closed the door behind me, making sure not to wake up my father and mother. "Good Morning guys, did you bring your backpacks?" I whispered. The boys turned around to show me that they had their backpacks. "Good, did you both leave notes telling your folks that we went daybreak fishing, and we would be back before dark?" I asked both.

"Yes," They both responded in a faint voice.

"Good, now let us get out of town while it is still dark and before everyone in town wakes up, we need to get to our tree fort.

"Except for the gate keeper," remarked Sammy.

The three of us boys walked as fast as we could on the only road in Munchkin town until we came to the front gates of the tall wall that was built to keep out wild animals and flying monkeys.

"It looks like the gate keeper is on a break, let's hurry up and climb over the wall before he returns." I stated.

Sammy quickly took off his backpack and pulled out a long rope that had a large fishing hook tied to one end. He started to spin the rope around a few times, and then he aimed at the top of the wall. The wall was almost twenty feet tall. Sammy tossed the rope upwards, it went over the wall, he then pulled on the rope until the hook caught the edge of the wall, "Alright, let's climb." Sammy said.

Ray-Ray was the first to start climbing up the rope, followed by me and then Sammy. Once we reached the top of the wall, Sammy pulled up the rope and dropped it down the other side. It was just a few minutes before the three of us boys climbed down and were on the ground outside the town walls.

"So far, so good," I said. "Now let's get to the tree fort."

We walked fast and soon reached a large old tree that was out of site and sounds from the town. The tree was tall with many thick branches and in the middle of it was a homemade fort built by us, it was tall enough for us to stand up in, it was almost five feet high, and it circled around the tree.

A rope ladder was attached to the bottom of the fort, I grabbed the rope ladder, "I will hold it while Ray-Ray climbs up and pops open the trap door to get in." I said.

Ray-Ray started to climb the twenty wooden steps that were tied into the long rope just a foot apart from each other. It took him a few minutes to reach the last step and the trap door of the fort, he climbed up and inside the fort, looked down at me and Sammy,

"Come on up, boys!" Sammy and I smiled up at him then Sammy started to climb, once he reached the top, I started to climb and soon made my way up the ladder. Soon all three of us were in the fort. I closed and locked the trap door after me, so no one could enter.

Once the trap door was secure, we sat down in our chairs, we looked at each other for a minute, and then I said, "Now that we are in our fort, we can talk about our plans, and eat some breakfast before we go."

CHAPTER 2

THE LOLLIPOP KIDS CLUB

WE TOOK OFF OUR BACKPACKS and pulled out a breakfast bag that we made at home the night before and also a jug that held our favorite drink, Munchkin punch. As we were starting to eat our food, I said, "We are all alone up here, nobody can hear about our plans."

"You mean the Evil Witch of the East or her spies that watch us and report back to her?" Ray-Ray inquired.

"Yes, if anyone of her spies heard about our plan, we wouldn't have a chance at all," replied Sammy.

"Boy! If my dad only knew what we were going to do, he would hit my backside so hard you all would feel it too! I joked. We all started laughing at my joke, they had no idea that a large Raven was flying over the same tree and heard their laughter. He dove down to a branch near an opening and landed on it making sure that the boys could not see him. Once there he watched and listened to what was making the boys laugh so hard.

Ray-Ray stood up holding his cup of Munchkin punch and happily stated, "Before we go over our plan, I want to give a toast to Jerry. Happy Birthday!"

Sammy stood up and cheered "Happy Birthday!"

I smiled at them, "Thanks guys but my birthday is tomorrow."

"Really?" Ray-Ray asked.

"I think I should know my own birthday." I answered.

"Oh well, so I am a day early." Ray-Ray responded.

Jerry raised his cup, "Thanks guys; I will toast to that also, this will be our first adventure of our new club we just started, The Lollipop Kids Club!"

The boys raised their cups in the air and cheered, "Lollipop Kids Club!" The boys drank from their cups and returned to their seats while I remained standing.

"Today we go to the castle of the Wicked Witch of the East and get her to follow us back here, so we can trap her and try to kill her!" I explained.

The Raven could not believe what he just overheard; those three boys are going to try to kill the Witch of the East. The Raven flapped his wings and flew straight up and out of the tree into the sun. Sammy saw the Raven; he watched as it flew east, the same way as the Wicked Witch of the East's castle was.

He then pointed out the Raven flying away to me and RayRay and remarked, "I think the Witch of the East will soon know about our plan!"

I watched the Raven, "Yes, I think that Raven is one of the Witches spies, we better get our weapons and pack them along with any other things we may need for our trip and get out of here while we can."

I walked over to a wooden chest that was in the corner of the room and opened it, inside were three special weapons. I reached inside and pulled out an enormous size lollipop that could be used as a shield or boomerang. Sammy was next, he reached in and pulled out a one hand glove and a throwing stone that had a rubber band attached to it, after the stone hits its target the stone returns into the special made glove. Ray-Ray was last and pulled out a bag filled with marbles and a hand-made sling shot. After we checked out our weapons, we packed them inside our backpacks.

"We are almost ready to go," I stated, "Let's checkout our traps we set before we leave."

Sammy walked over to a rope tied to the wall, he checked it out and made sure it was still tied to a bucket of water hanging from the ceiling, "This one is ready!"

Ray-Ray walked behind the trapped door and investigated a small box, "The fire sticks are here and ready to go."

"Good, it has been said that water or fire can kill an evil witch. I am sure who ever told that tale was telling the truth." I said.

"Do you really think our plan about stealing the Evil Witch of the East's magic wand and getting her so mad that she follows us back here will work? Ray-Ray questioned me.

"We won't know until we try my friend, now let's climb down and get started, we have a long way before we reach the border lands between the land of Good and Evil and the castle of the Wicked Witch of the East." I replied.

I then opened and held the trap door while Sammy and Ray-Ray started to climb down the rope ladder. I followed and took one more look at our club fort and thought to myself, "I sure hope this won't be the last time I ever see this place." I started to climb down the ladder, closing the trap door behind me. After I climbed down the three of us walked until we reached the road.

"We just follow the yellow brick road until it forks off to the East and the border land" I reminded the others. We only made it a few steps when we heard a woman's voice, "Good morning boys! May I ask where you are going this early?"

CHAPTER 3

RUBY, THE PARROT

MY FRIENDS AND I LOOKED up at a nearby tree. "Look it is a talking parrot," Ray-Ray said. We walked over to the tree,

I said, "Hello there, my friends and I thought we would go fishing this morning."

"Well hello boys, my name is Ruby, it is nice to meet you. May I ask how you boys are going fishing without any fishing poles?" Ruby wondered.

We all looked at each other, then Ray-Ray stated, "We are not going fishing but, on our way, to kill the Witch of the East."

Sammy quickly put his hand over Ray-Ray's mouth, "Be quiet, we don't know if she is another spy of the Witch."

"WHAT!" Ruby shouted, she flapped her wings saying, "Are you boys crazy?" She was the most beautiful looking parrot; she had a tiny gold chain that had a small pair of ruby shoes that sparkled in the sun.

"My name is Jerry, and my two friends are Sammy and Ray-Ray." I informed Ruby.

"We are not crazy," Sammy replied, "Why do you care? Are you a spy of hers?"

"No! That Evil Witch and her older sister are in fact enemies of mine," Ruby responded in a firm voice to them that she was not a spy for any evil witch. "I only said that before, because the Munchkins are good and peaceful people, and it would pain me if those witches killed any of them including the three boys standing in front of me."

"We are tired of seeing the Witch of the East making our people work her fields to feed those flying monkeys of hers and live in fear that she would cut off our water supply that comes from her evil land of the East."

Ruby was quiet for a moment, "I'm sorry boys, what you are about to try is the bravest thing I've heard of in a very long time."

"Thank you," I replied and asked, "How much do you know about that Witch anyway?"

Ruby looked at the boys and said, "I know that you boys are not the first ones to attempt to kill the Evil Witches of the East and West, in fact, the Witch has dungeons underneath her castle filled with many who have tried or just got her mad. I also know the Good Witches from the North and South have done battle with them in the past, but it always comes to a draw."

After Ruby was done, I asked, "Can you please excuse us, we need to talk between ourselves."

"It is alright with me," Ruby responded.

We turned away and whispered amongst ourselves. "I think it would be a good idea if we ask her to help us," I said.

"I feel that the parrot is very special, I like her," remarked Ray-Ray.

"Well, if you all want her to join our club, I am fine with it. "We need all the help we can get," spoke Sammy. The boys turned back and looked at Ruby.

"Would you go with us to the Witch of the Easts castle?" I asked her nervously.

Ruby just looked at the three of us without saying a word, then she answered, "If I say no, there is three fewer Munchkins, so I guess my answer will be YES! I will go with you boys and do what I can to help out." She then flew down onto Ray-Ray's shoulder, "I will ride with you for a while." We all cheered.

I said, "We have another club member." The group of four started to walk along the yellow brick road together.

"May I ask you boys what kind of club I now belong to?" Ruby inquired.

"It is called the Lollipop Kids Club," answered Ray-Ray.

"Oh, may I ask another question? What is a lollipop?" Ruby asked.

The three of us laughed while I reached into my pants pocket and pulled out one of my homemade lollipops, I unwrapped it and put it in front of her.

She looked at it with a puzzled look then she took it and licked it. "WOW! This is good Jerry," she remarked.

"Thanks, that one is made from bananas," Jerry proudly answered.

"Now you know why we call Jerry the lollipop kid, he makes the best lollipops in all the lands," The boys explained.

"I think I am going to like being a member of your club," Ruby replied. The boys laughed while walking and continued towards the castle of the Witch of the East. After Ruby was finished, she said, now that I am a member of this club, can you tell me more about your plans?"

"Sure," I answered her, "We sneak into her castle, find her magic wand and steal it, get her so mad at us that she follows us back to our clubhouse tree fort, once there, we set up our traps, killing her and setting our people free of her forever."

Ruby started to laugh, after a few moments she said, "That is your plan, go steal her magic wand, get her mad so she follows all of you back to Munchkin town, so you can trap and kill her?"

We all thought about what she just said, we all started to laugh, soon all four members were laughing at the plan. After a while, the boys stopped laughing and Sammy asked, "Why are we laughing?"

"Because the Witch is always mad! She is going to come after you boys without stealing her magic wand!" chuckled Ruby.

The three of us did not think about that and remained quiet and thought about what Ruby just said.

CHAPTER 4

CASTLES OF THE WITCH OF THE EAST & WEST

MEANWHILE, ON THE OTHER side of the border land where only evil is welcome, the Raven that overheard the boys earlier was still flying towards his master's castle. "There it is," he told himself. Raven looked at the mountain ahead of him. The Witches' castle was built into the side of the mountain; it stood over ten stories high with a ton of watch towers and a stone wall that protected it from anyone that may try to attack. The Raven flew down towards an open window and into the castle, he entered, "Master, Master, where are you?"

"I am here!" A voice shouted out from one of the dozens of rooms that were inside her castle. The Raven listened to the voice and followed it until he flew into the room it was coming from. Inside the room the Raven flew over to a bird stand and landed on it.

"Master, I have news!" Raven said flapping his wings.

The Witch was in the center of the room standing over a large cooking pot stirring it over a small fire. She was tall, wearing a long black dress with a black cape attached to the back of it, and a pointed cone hat with long black boots. She was green and mean to anyone that had any good in them. "One minute my pet, I don't want to burn my potions," she explained to him. After a few more stirs with her large spoon, she stopped and walked over to the Raven, "What kind of news do you bring me?" She then picked him up and looked into his eyes and read his mind. After a moment she said, "So, three Munchkin boys are coming here to kill me." The Evil Witch slowly developed a grin on her face. "This is some of the best news I heard in over a hundred years." The Evil Witch put the Raven on the bird stand, "You did very good, my pet." She pulled out her magic wand from underneath her cape and waved it at the table near the bird stand, a large plate filled with every type of food a Raven would love to eat appeared. The Raven flapped his wings with excitement and jumped onto the table and started to enjoy his reward.

The Captain of the flying monkeys came running in the room, "Master is everything all right? I heard the sounds of trouble." He was covered with short hair, stood five feet tall, walked mostly on two legs, had wings strong enough to carry something much heavier than him and he was dressed in his battle uniform. Besides him there were over two hundred flying monkeys that lived in the castle that made up the Witches of the East army.

"Yes!" The Witch answered, "The castle will soon be attacked, we are about to be attacked by three Munchkin boys."

The flying monkey stopped and looked at the Witch, "Did you say three Munchkins are coming to our castle to attack us!?!"

"Yes!" The Evil Witch responded, and then started to laugh. The flying monkeys started to laugh along with her, along with the Raven who was still eating his reward. A few more flying monkeys came into the room after hearing about the Munchkin boys, they laughed so hard they fell. After a few more minutes, the Witch stopped laughing, "I need to call my sister, you three come with me to the map and crystal ball room." She walked out of the spell and potion room and upstairs, down the long hallway into another room, the three flying monkeys were close behind her. This was the map and crystal ball room in which the Evil Witch could call and see her older sister the Wicked Witch of the West, also one of the walls in the room had a painted picture of all the land of the East, West, North and South. The map also showed the border between the lands of the Witch of the East and the town of Munchkin.

A glowing light could be seen coming from an enormous size crystal ball in the middle of the room. A small fireplace burned and beside that was a table with two wooden chairs. Once inside the Witch walked over to the crystal ball, two flying monkeys pulled out a chair. The Witch of the East sat down and placed both hands on the crystal ball, "Sister, Sister, are you there?" The Witch spoke as she looked into the crystal ball in front of her, suddenly a fog appeared.

"Hello sister! What can I do for you?" The Witch of the West said.

"I was told by my spy that three Munchkin boys have left the safety of their town and are now on their way here to kill me." The Witch of the East stated curtly.

The face inside the crystal ball began to laugh and laugh for the next few minutes, then she stopped, "That is the funniest thing I ever heard in my long life!" The Witch of the West laughed.

"I know!" The Witch of the East answered her sister, "But it is true, I think you should fly over here, this may be the chance we have been waiting for, to trap the Good Witches."

"Sounds like fun, I will fly over after I take care of some things." The Witch of the West responded chuckling.

The face of the Witch of the West disappeared back into the fog and was gone.

The Witch of the East stood up and looked at the three flying monkeys standing beside her, "You two, go up to the roof and wait for my sister, when she gets here bring her here to me."

"Yes, master," they responded. The two flying monkeys turned and ran out of the room towards the roof while the Captain stayed with the Witch, She walked over to the wall map and started to study it, looking for a place where a trap could be set to capture and kill a Good Witch.

Meanwhile, In the land to the West, the Wicked Witch of the West was inside her castle. It stood on top of a mountain, it was just as large as her sister's, with many watch towers, had over two hundred flying monkeys guarding it.

The Witch was busy mixing a special potion, "A little bit of this and a pinch of that will make a monster for all to fear," She sang. She took a clear bottle from her hand and waved her magic wand over it, then she stuck a cork in it; placed it in one of her pockets inside her cape, then yelled "Broom, come to me!!" The broom was downstairs on the other side of the castle when it heard its master's orders. It lifted and started to fly towards the Witch, as it flew it hit anything that came into its way including a few flying monkeys. Within a few minutes it reached the Witch and landed beside her. The Witch grabbed the broom and told the Captain beside her, "I think I have everything!"

"What are your orders, Master?" The Captain asked.

"I want you to take half the flying monkeys to the far side of the land of the North and attack the town." The Witch of the West told him.

"That town is protected by the Good Witch of the North and her army of Bear-man," responded the Captain.

"Yes, I know that" replied the Witch of the West. "I am counting on her to come to their rescue and be away so only one Good Witch is around to fight when the time comes to set our trap. Once you see the Good Witch of the North and her Bear-man army, retreat back to the border land between the land of the East and South near Munchkin town."

"Yes, master!" The Captain responded. He ran out of the room letting out a loud scream that alarmed every flying monkey in the castle, they knew that sound was the call for battle and to get to the roof top and wait for their master.

A few minutes later the Captain climbed the long stairway that led up to the roof top. He opened the door and saw hundreds of flying monkeys standing on the roof of the castle and the walls waiting for their master. The Captain walked into the center of them and yelled, "Master's orders is to have half of our army fly with me while the rest of you stay here and wait for her. Now, every other one of you soldiers fly with me," then he jumped off the castle wall flapping his wings. He flew straight up into the sky towards the land of the North followed by over a hundred flying monkeys.

A few more minutes went by, and the roof top door opened again, this time the Witch of the West walked out. She walked over to where the rest of the flying monkeys were standing.

"My pet's, today we fly to the castle of the Witch of the East and trap three Munchkin boys and kill a Good Witch, if we are lucky." The flying monkeys cheered with excitement. The Witch sat on her broom, "Fly! To my sister's castle." The broom took off into the sky along with a hundred of her flying monkeys heading eastward.

Meantime, back at the castle of the Witch of the East, two flying monkeys were still on the roof top of the castle waiting for the Wicked Witch of the West to arrive. "How long before our master's sister gets here?" One of the flying monkeys asked the other.

"I don't know, she can fly really fast with that broom of hers," The other one answered.

"Do you think our master will finally defeat those Good Witches this time?" remarked the flying monkey as he kept an eye on the sky above.

"I don't know, those four Witches have been fighting for hundreds of years, maybe this time our master will kill them," The other flying monkey replied.

Down a few levels of the castle the Witch of the East was still studying the map wall, "There! The spot we can set a trap and kill those Good Witches," she said.

The Captain of the flying monkeys looked at the map where she was pointing, "How are you going to get those Good Witches to cross over into the forbidden zone to our land of evil?"

"Do not worry, my pet. This is why my sister is coming over," she answered, "Between her and I, we will think of something to get them to cross over!" A bell started to sound from one of the castle's watch towers, the Witch heard the bell, "That is the sound I have been waiting for, my sister must be arriving."

One of the flying monkeys was ringing the bell as the other one shouted, "The Witch of the West is arriving, and she brought part of her army with her."

In the sky above the castle the Witch of the West was flying, circling with her army. She looked down below and saw the flying monkeys waving to her, she pointed them and shouted, "Follow me!" She dove down towards the flying monkeys and landed beside them. Her army of flying monkeys started to land on top of the roof and walls of the castle.

"Hello master and welcome, your sister is waiting for you down below in the map room, if you please follow me, I will take you to her," spoke one of the flying monkeys that was waiting for her.

The Witch of the West looked at her army of flying monkeys, "All of you stay here and wait while I go talk to my sister."

The two flying monkeys went to the stairway leading down into the castle, they both held out light torches and started walking down the steps. The Wicked Witch of the West followed them holding her broom. After a few levels they reached a door, the two flying monkeys opened it, "We are here," and they walked down the hallway and entered the room.

"Hello, come over here my dear sister, I've got something to show you," said the Witch of the East.

The two Witches hugged one another. "It has been much too long since we saw each other," remarked the Witch of the East to her older sister.

"Yes, I know," answered the Witch of the West. "Now, that I am here, tell me what is going on?"

"I believe we have been given a chance to do something we have been trying to do for hundreds of years! Kill those two Good Witches of the North and South," stated the Witch of the East.

"That is what I was thinking also!" The Witch of the West said laughing.

"Well, the three Munchkin boys left their homes before dawn and will be walking the yellow brick road until they reach the fork in the road," The Witch of the East said as she pointed with her wand at the map on the wall. "They must pass by the Munchkin farmers pumpkin patch along the way. What do you think about setting a trap to catch the boys and use them as bait to kill a Good Witch or two?"

The Witch of the West looked at the map wall in front of her for a minute, "Yes, sister, I like your plan and I think we must get one of the Good Witches to cross over into the forbidden zone to our evil land, once there her powers will fade quickly and then we can kill her! I brought a special potion with me that will help get three Munchkin boys and take them to a spot across the border and hold them prisoners until the Good Witch tries to free them."

The Witch of the East smiled at her sister, "I want to battle the Good Witch of the South!"

"Alright with me," replied the Witch of the West. "I will take the Good Witch of the North!" Then she pulled out the clear bottle from inside her cape pocket that carried her special potion mix, "This will help us in our plan," she showed it to her sister.

The Witch of the East looked at it and smiled, "What does it do?"

The Witch of the West pointed to the pumpkin patch on the wall map, "I will unleash a monster that will bring those boys where we wish." She looked at the Captain of the flying monkeys, handed him the bottle and told him, "Take this to the farmers pumpkin patch and find the scarecrow, once you find him pour this over his head and tell it to bring those Munchkin boys to this spot." The Captain looked as the Witch of the West pointed to a spot across the forbidden zone on the evil land. "But whatever you do, don't get him mad," remarked the Witch of the West.

"Yes, Master as you ordered," answered the Captain. He took the bottle from her and put it inside his uniform jacket pocket, he then ran towards an open window and jumped out. He was soon flying fast towards the Munchkin farmer's pumpkin patch. The Witch of the East laughed just thinking about what kind of monster her sister was going to make.

"I also ordered half of my army to fly to the Good Witch of the North's land and attack the town on the far side, so she and her Bear-man army will go there to help, that will leave only one Good Witch against both of us!" The Witch of the West told her sister. "Now all we have to do is wait until we here from our spies.

"I like to add one more thing to our plan," spoke the Witch of the West, she pointed her wand and waved it at the wall map towards the pumpkin patch; "Give me a storm to slow down the Munchkins while the Captain visits Mr. Scarecrow!" Then the two Witches walked over to the table and sat down, made themselves a mug of witches' brew and waited for news to come.

MICHAEL T ERNST

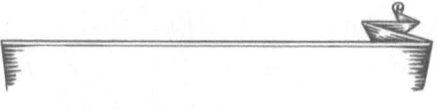

CHAPTER 5

PUMPKIN PATCH

THE MUNCHKINS AND RUBY were still walking on the yellow brick road. "Hey, Ruby may I ask you a question?" Ray-Ray spoke as he looked at her.

"Sure, go ahead and ask," Ruby answered.

"Why do you have a tiny pair of ruby colored shoes attached to that necklace around your neck?" Ray-Ray asked.

"I am a lady, and you never know when a good pair of shoes will be needed," Ruby answered.

The three of us looked at her and were puzzled by her response but said nothing more about her ruby shoes.

Ruby then raised her neck in the air and shouted, "I smell pumpkins!" She flapped her wings, "Last one there is a rotten egg!" She then jumped off Ray-Ray's shoulders and flew straight ahead to a large farmers pumpkin patch.

"You heard the lady," I said, I started to run following Ruby. Sammy and Ray-Ray started to run after him, each one trying not to get to the pumpkin patch last. The pumpkin patch has many acres, it stretched along the yellow brick road and over the small hill. A few minutes of running I finally caught up with Ruby, she was sitting on a large pumpkin picking out seeds and eating them,

"Boy, I sure love pumpkin seeds," Ruby said.

I sat down next to her, Sammy was next to arrive, and Ray-Ray came running up behind him. The boys sat down and tried to catch their breath while Ruby enjoyed her pumpkin seeds.

"I guess this is a good place to take a lunch break," I said to everyone. I took off my backpack to grab my lunch out of it. Sammy and Ray-Ray did the same thing. Soon all four were enjoying their lunch, laughing about Ray-Ray smelling like a rotten egg. We did not know about the danger coming our way.

We were still enjoying a lunch break when Ruby suddenly stopped eating and looked up at the blue sky, "A storm is coming, we better find shelter."

We looked up and Sammy said, "There is not a cloud in the sky." It was not long after that when a dark cloud appeared in the sky just above the hill ahead of them.

I noticed the farmers barn just a short distance to the side of us. "Let's get to that barn before the storm comes." I said, pointing at the barn a short distance away.

We quickly ran as fast as we could towards the barn. The storm hit, winds started to blow hard, and the rain came, it was hot and burned us as we ran inside the open barn door. I shut the barn door once everyone was safely inside.

"WOW! That rain was so hot it burned," remarked RayRay.

"Yea, what kind of rain burns like that?" Sammy asked.

"Evil Witches rain!" Ruby answered.

"What? How do you know that?" I asked.

"Trust me, I know," said Ruby, "She must know about your plans, and this is her way of telling you."

"What do we do now?" Sammy inquired.

"We wait out the storm inside this barn until it is over," I replied. We all waited inside the barn while just on the other side of the hill the sun was shining.

The flying monkey Captain was the fastest flyer in the Witches army and soon was flying over the farmer's pumpkin field, "There you are," he said to himself and quickly dove down and landed beside the tall scarecrow. He walked around it, checking it out, it was tied to a wooden fence pole, and stuffed with hay and sticks, had a pair of farmer's overalls and long sleeve shirt, and had a pumpkin placed on top of it in place of a head.

"Boy, you are sure one ugly scarecrow." He then climbed up onto the top of the scarecrow, he reached inside his jacket pocket and pulled out the bottle with the Witches potion in it, "Mr. Scarecrow time to wake up," he opened the bottle and poured it over the pumpkin head then jumped off.

It only took a moment before the whole scarecrow began to shake then its overalls started to fill out along with his chest and the rest of his body, the hay, branches and sticks now turned into blood and bones; his hands and feet formed claws and two blood-colored eyes appeared on the pumpkin head along with an evil grin. Suddenly it jumped straight up breaking the ropes that held him and landed a few feet away from the flying monkey, who fell backwards to the ground and now was looking up at two red angry eyes,

"Why do I live," asked the Scarecrow.

"Back off you freak!" Yelled the Captain at him as he slowly stood up.

The Scarecrow took one step backwards; he did not like the tone of the flying monkey.

"I will tell you why you live, because our master has a job for you," the Captain explained to him.

"Who is our master and what is the job?" The Scarecrow asked, confused.

"The Witches of the East and West are your masters, and they want you to grab three Munchkin boys that will be coming this way and bring them across the Good land into the Evil land," the Captain explained further.

"But why?" The Scarecrow asked.

"Stop asking me so many questions, you oversized pumpkin pie!" The Captain shouted at him. The Scarecrow had about enough of the Captain's tone and was getting mad at him. "Now, stop asking me questions, do as you are ordered, go over to the yellow brick road and wait for those Munchkins," The Captain told the Scarecrow.

The Scarecrow asked another question, "What is my name?"

The Captain looked at him, "How about Scary Pumpkin? NOW MOVE IT!

"I only have one more question for you," said Scary Pumpkin.

The Captain looked at him, "What is your question?"

"Tell me, what do monkeys taste like?" Scary Pumpkin asked.

The Captain just remembered what the Witch of the West told him, 'Don't get him mad!!' The Captain slowly stepped back from him saying, "Do not even think about it! We are on the same side."

Scary Pumpkin took a step closer to the Captain and gave him an evil grin. The Captain knew he made a terrible mistake; he turned and jumped into the air flapping his wings, trying to get away from him. The flying monkey did not have a chance to get away, Scary Pumpkin jumped high into the air and caught him while he was attempting to fly away. The Captain screamed in pain as he was ripped in half by Scary Pumpkin's razor-sharp claws, his bloody body fell back to the ground. Scary Pumpkin landed beside him and looked at the dead flying monkey,

"It is time to find out what monkey taste like." Scary Pumpkin exclaimed!

After a few minutes, Scary Pumpkin looked down at what was left of the Captain, he picked up the only thing remaining, the tail of a flying monkey, he stuck it in his back pocket and said, "Not too bad! Now let us see what a Munchkin taste like." He stood up and walked over to the yellow brick road, once there he sat down in the middle of it and waited for three Munchkin boys.

Meantime, on the other side of the hill, Ruby and us boys were still waiting for the Witches storm to end. After a little while of waiting, the storm ended, and the sun appeared.

I happily spoke, "Now let's get going before anything else happens!" I opened the barn door; Ruby flew out of the barn and up the hill and landed on a tree. The three of us made our way back to the yellow brick road and started up the hill toward Ruby.

"What is she waiting for?" Ray-Ray asked.

"I don't know," I answered. We reached the top of the hill and now knew what Ruby was waiting for, it was the most frightening looking thing that we had ever seen before.

"What is that thing down there?" Ray-Ray asked nervously.

"It is evil and works for the Witches," Ruby answered.

"How are we going to get by that thing!" Sammy said in a worried tone.

"Well boys, this is what I like to say is a fork in the road," Ruby remarked.

"What do you mean, Ruby?" I asked.

"Well boys, you have two choices, you can turn around and go home and be safe or you can go down there and face that thing. If you choose this way, one of the Lollipop Kid's Club members will be killed and another will end up in the Witch's dungeons." Ruby explained.

We all looked at Ruby and I said, "How do you know that?"

"I can't tell you that at this time but trust me," Ruby replied.

I faced Sammy and Ray-Ray, "Well you guys, what do you think?"

"If we don't try, our loved ones will never be free!" Sammy spoke up quickly.

"I think we can still defeat that Evil Witch some way and I am ready to die trying!" Ray-Ray stated matter-of fact.

"I am with you, my friends! Let us go down there and defeat that thing! I said then shouted, "MUNCHKIN POWER!!" All three of us raised our hands together in the air.

Ruby looked at the boys and smiled at them, "You boys are very brave, I am glad to be a member of this club." She then flew onto my shoulder, "Let's go boys!"

All of us quickly took out our weapons and slowly walked towards the monster waiting for them in the middle of the road. As Ruby, the boys and I made it down the hill, That thing saw us and stood up.

We aimed our weapons at him and got ready to shoot when Ruby said, "Stop here."

We did as Ruby said and stopped; and we stood in place. Ruby whispered to us, "Do you mind if I handle this matter?"

We looked at her, nodded our heads yes; we were too scared to speak after seeing the monster up close.

CHAPTER 6

SCARY PUMPKIN

THE MONSTER LOOKED at them," My name is Scary Pumpkin and I'm looking for the Munchkins," and then he opened his mouth showing off his large white teeth that still had blood stains on them. Ruby opened her wings, the tiny Ruby shoes started to glow, then from underneath her wings a beam of light shot out towards Scary Pumpkin's red eyes blinding him. Scary Pumpkin fell to his knees holding his eyes. We all just watched Scary Pumpkin. We looked at Ruby wondering what was going on.

Suddenly Scary Pumpkin stood up and removed his hands from his eyes, opened them and they were now yellow.

Scary Pumpkin said, "Hello there, can we be friends?" We could not believe our ears; we lowered our weapons and looked at Ruby.

Ruby looked at us and winked and speaking in a soft and calm tone spoke to Scary Pumpkin, "Yes, my friends and I would like that; in fact, we would like you to join our club and come with us. My name is Ruby, and this is our club leader Jerry and his two best friends Sammy and RayRay."

"Hello, Mr. Scary Pumpkin," we all said together.

Scary Pumpkin looked at us and asked, "Are you guys called Munchkins?"

"Yes, we are," I answered.

"Oh, I heard about you. I cannot remember why though but I would like to join your club and go with you." Scary Pumpkin replied.

"Good!" I said to Scary Pumpkin, "Our club is called the Lollipop Kids Club, and we are going on our first club adventure."

"I have two questions," said Scary Pumpkin looking at the boys and Ruby, "What is a lollipop and where are we going?"

"I will be happy to answer your questions," I replied. I reached into my pants pocket and pulled out a lollipop and handed it to him, "This is called a lollipop; it is candy that I made myself."

Scary Pumpkin looked at it, opened his mouth and tossed it in swallowing it whole, "Not bad, now where are we going?"

"We are going to an Evil Witches castle to steal her magic wand, then we are going back to our club tree fort," I answered.

"Okay with me, let's go!" Scary Pumpkin said and started to walk along the yellow brick road leading the way. We looked at Ruby again trying to understand what she did to him, she just looked back at us and gave another wink.

While we walked, Sammy said, "Now we are five strong!"

Ray-Ray noticed something hanging out of the back pocket of Scary Pumpkin's overalls, "Hey, Mr. Scary Pumpkin, what is that sticking out of your pocket?"

Scary Pumpkin reached behind him and pulled it out, looking at it without missing a step, "I don't know, I can't remember but it looks like something I ate."

"It looks like a part of a flying monkey," I remarked.

"Yes, indeed, that is the tail of a flying monkey, I've seen many in my time," Ruby replied.

"Boy! The Witch is going to be mad at you for eating one of her flying monkeys," replied Sammy.

"So, what does monkey taste like anyway?" I inquired.

Scary Pumpkin put the tail in his mouth and chewed it, then replied, "It taste kind of funny."

"Well, the Witch won't think it is funny," laughed Ruby.

Scary Pumpkin and us boys started to laugh along with her and continued walking along the yellow brick road.

CHAPTER 7

THIRTEEN FLYING MONKEYS TO GO

BACK INSIDE THE CASTLE of the Witch of the East both evil sisters were still waiting for news from the Captain of the flying monkeys. "Tell me sister, what is taking your Captain so long?" The Witch of the West questioned.

"I don't know, he is my fastest flying monkey in my entire army, he should have been here by now!" The Witch of the East replied.

"I have a bad feeling that something has happened to him, maybe we should send out some more flying monkeys," remarked the Witch of the West.

"Good idea," replied the Witch of the East, she ordered a nearby flying monkey to come to her, "I want you to fly to the farmers pumpkin patch, take a dozen flying monkeys with you and find out what happened to the Captain."

"That is good thinking sister, I am sure that a pack of flying monkeys will find out what is going on," replied the Witch of the West.

"Do you think your army has started to attack the town in the North yet?" The Witch of the East asked.

The Witch of the West looked outside the window at the afternoon sun, "Very soon," she commented.

"Good, it won't be long after before the Good Witch of the North and her army of Bear-man will leave their castle to save that town," cackled the Witch of the East.

"Yes, everything is going as planned, all we have to do is wait a little longer and when the sun sets today and the moon rises beaming its hollow eve night our power will be at its strongest all year," remarked the Witch of the West, "Then we will kill a Good Witch or two," she laughed.

The flying monkey ran outside the castle to a pack of nearby flying monkeys, "Our master has ordered me and one dozen of you to fly to find the missing Captain."

One dozen flying monkeys took a step towards him and in one loud voice said, "Let's go find our brother!"

"Good, follow me to the farmer's pumpkin patch," said the first flying monkey, then he jumped into the air and started flying the same way the Captain did, the dozen flying monkeys were soon in the air close behind him.

It was late afternoon in the North land; the flying monkeys were flying high and getting close to the town ordered by the Witch of the West to attack.

The Captain looked at the flying monkey beside him, "Fly down to one of those trees and wait, when you see any signs of the Good Witch, or those Bear-man come quick and warn us."

"Yes, Captain," the flying monkey answered and dove down to the closest tree and landed on a thick branch to wait.

A loud bell started to sound; it was a special bell that the Good Witch made long ago. It was special because it rang in town and rang a bell that was inside the castle of the Good Witch of the North.

"Did you hear that?" One of the flying monkeys asked.

"Yes, it is the bell, the town knows we are coming, also the Good Witch of the North," replied the Captain, "Attack the town until we get word that the Good witch is coming to save the town, then we get out of here fast before those Bear-man can catch us! NOW FOLLOW ME!" The Captain shouted and dove towards the town followed by a hundred of his brothers.

A speaker box that was placed on top of the tallest building came on and a voice came through, "Flying monkeys are about to attack, stay in your homes and lock the doors! We called for help! The Good Witch will be here as soon as she can!" Those were the last words the speaker box spoke; a flying monkey ripped it off the roof top. The sounds of screams and things breaking could be heard throughout the entire town.

Back at the Good Witch of the North's castle, Bear-man came running up to the Good Witch, "My Good Witch, the warning bell from the town near the border of the Wicked Witch of the West is sending out an alarm!"

The Good Witch, who was the oldest and the wisest of all four witches; was sitting in her favorite room in the castle, which was in the middle of a large valley, it was beautifully made out of white granite with stone walls around it with over a dozen tall cone shaped towers with many rooms. It was protected by her army of Bear-man. The Bear-man stood over nine feet tall and had the body of a large bear and the head of a man. "Tell the army to be ready to go in two minutes and bring my unicorn to the front gates of the castle," ordered the Good Witch of the North.

"Yes, my Good Witch," the Bear-man replied, he quickly ran out of the room, so he could do as he was ordered.

The Good Witch of the North wondered as she prepared herself for battle, "It has been a long time since the Evil Witches attacked any towns, I wonder why they started now."

In moments, dozens of Bear-men stood in front of the castle waiting for the Good Witch, the large front gates of the castle opened, the Good Witch walked out and over to her army and unicorn. "The alarm bell ringing means the Evil Witch crossed over into the good land and is attacking our friends," the Good Witch said.

The Captain of the Bear-man army asked, "What are your orders?"

The Good Witch climbed up onto her white unicorn, "We ride as fast as we can to save our friends!"

The unicorn raised up on two legs then started to run, the Bear-man army also started to run on all four legs.

CHAPTER 8

BEWARE OF THE LOST WOODS

BACK ON THE YELLOW brick road the Lollipop Club members reached a bend in the road. A sign on a pole read, "THIS WAY TO THE LOST WOODS AND WITCHES CASTLE. ENTER AT YOUR OWN RISK!"

Ruby was on Scary Pumpkin's shoulder and remarked after reading the sign, "If we stay on the yellow brick road it will take us to Emerald City, we must take the path that leads into the Lost Woods to get to her castle."

"Boy, I heard lots of bad things about these woods, like once you enter your lost forever and evil creatures chase you the rest of your life!" Sammy remarked.

"Well boys there are more dangerous things out there," replied Ruby.

"What could be worse?" Ray-Ray inquired.

Ruby smiled and pointed one of her wings at Scary Pumpkin. We looked at him, Scary Pumpkin opened his mouth showing off his bloody teeth again and said, "Don't worry, my friends, I will take care of any monster that comes our way," then he walked off the yellow brick road and started to follow a pathway in the dirt that led to the Lost Woods dead ahead. The three of us boys did not say another word, just followed him single file, walking on the same footsteps Scary Pumpkin made with his claw feet. It was not a long walk before Scary Pumpkin reached the tree line of the Lost Woods; he slowly entered the thick woods making sure to cut a pathway for the Munchkins to follow. I was behind him; Sammy was next then Ray-Ray was last in line. Scary Pumpkin only made it a short way into the woods when his head and body started to shake. Ruby looked at him wondering what was wrong. Then she heard a noise coming from behind her, she turned to see what it was but only us three boys were there, just a few feet away, walking in line.

Suddenly, she knew what and who made that sound, "Oh my!" She told herself, "I think it would be a good time to go get some fresh air and find more help." She jumped off Scary Pumpkin and into the air saying, "I will be back soon, keep going!"

We watched as she flew away, out of site. I was only a few feet away from Scary Pumpkin when I grabbed my nose saying, "I know why Ruby left," and continued to hold my nose as I walked.

"Where did she go?" Ray-Ray inquired, "Never mind!" as the smell reached him, and he grabbed his nose.

"What are you guys talking about?" Sammy asked who was the last one walking in line.

"Oh, you will find out soon," I snickered with my nose plugged.

"Oh man! What in the name of Oz is that nasty smell?" Sammy asked, as he grabbed his nose.

Scary Pumpkin turned his head around while still walking forward and responded, "What are you boys talking about?"

"Can't you smell that," I asked Scary Pumpkin.

"Do you see a nose on this Pumpkin head," Scary Pumpkin asked. All three of us boys nodded our heads no. "I am sorry my friends, I didn't mean to pass gas, it must have been something I ate."

"Yes, it is that flying monkey!" Ray-Ray answered.

Oh yea! That must be it." Scary Pumpkin said as he remembered.

"Hey, how can you turn your head around while still walking straight ahead," I asked.

Scary Pumpkin looked at us boys and said, "What! You all cannot do it."

"No, we cannot," we all responded.

"Have you tried?" Scary Pumpkin asked then he started laughing.

"Hey, the big guy has a sense of humor," Sammy remarked while joining him in the laughter.

Soon all the boys joined in on the laughter.

They were all laughing so hard when suddenly Scary Pumpkin said, "Oh No! Not again," he lowered his head and looked at the back of his overalls; they started blowing up like a balloon.

I watched his overalls and said, "Guys, you are not going to believe this," pointing at Scary Pumpkins backside.

"WOW, I think he is going to blow! EVERYONE TAKE COVER," shouted Ray-Ray. The three of us boys dove out of the way under some bushes, Scary Pumpkin passed gas so hard it popped open the flap on his backside of his overalls and shot him straight up like a rocket past the treetops, he fell back to the ground hard on his two feet.

"Please, boys don't make me laugh again," Scary Pumpkin begged.

We all came out of the bushes promising that we would not make him laugh. Scary Pumpkin reached into one of his many pockets and found a piece of string; he looked at the open flap and used the string to tie it close again. "That is better," he said when he was finished and started walking again. He only took a few steps then stopped dead in his tracks, "Something is watching us! You all wait here while I find out who is out there," Scary Pumpkin whispered.

"Alright," I responded quietly.

Scary Pumpkin started walking deeper into the Lost Woods as he did the sun faded and soon, he was in darkness, but that did not slow him down, in fact he saw things better in the dark.

He smiled an evil grin and shouted, "COME OUT! COMEOUT! WHO EVER YOU ARE!" Shortly after he saw pairs of pink glowing eyes appear in the darkness all around him moving closer. Scary Pumpkin could see them, they were a mix breed of creatures, part big Leopard and part big Lizard, they had pin shaped teeth, were over six feet long, had a long tail with spikes sticking out of them, their skin was as tough as steel.

Out from the darkness a lady's voice came, "GET HIM GIRLS!" Two creatures jumped out from behind a large tree and started running at him, Scary Pumpkin just stood in place and waited for them, still smiling with that evil grin. They jumped straight at him with their mouths wide open, showing their teeth. Scary Pumpkin lifted both hands up and caught them in midair with his claws. Another two creatures attacked him from behind, he turned his head around.

"I do not think so! Scary Pumpkin said as he lifted one of his legs up and used it like a bat swinging at them just before they reached him, both were hit at the same time, they flew backwards out of site. Another two attacked his legs that was supporting him, knocking him to the ground. Scary Pumpkin tried to stand up, but he could not, those creatures were holding both his legs. So, he raised both arms, and when he did two more creatures jumped on him pinning him down. One creature jumped onto his chest and looked into his yellow eyes with her pink ones.

"My name is Ginger, leader of the pack of Leopard Lizards, what kind of creature are you?" Ginger asked.

"I am a mad creature! My name is Scary Pumpkin; now let me up before you really get me mad."

CHAPTER 9

LEOPARD LIZARDS

"WELL, I CAN UNDERSTAND why they call you Scary Pumpkin, now let's get some things straight," Ginger said in a low tone to his face. "You and the three boys are in our woods trespassing."

"I'm only going to say this one more time," Scary Pumpkin said, "RELEASE ME NOW! Or all of you will see just how scary I can be!"

Ginger smiled at him, "You know, when you get mad, you are kind of cute."

"That is, it!" Scary Pumpkin said, he turned both of his wrists and hands around, his claws shot out enough for him to grab both Leopard Lizards, and with his great strength he threw them high into the treetops. Then he used his feet like hands and grabbed the two Leopard Lizards holding both his legs, he now used his legs kicking them into a nearby tree. After seeing what just happened to four Leopard Lizards, Ginger wanted no part of Scary Pumpkin. She jumped off his chest, but she was not fast enough for Scary Pumpkin's quick reflexes, he caught her with both hands by the neck, he then stood straight up and looked her in the eyes.

"I warned you not to get me mad, but you didn't listen; now it is going to cost you." He then started to choke her.

"STOP! Let her go came a boy's voice from behind him. Scary Pumpkin turned to see me standing there with Sammy and Ray-Ray looking at him.

"Hey guys, I didn't call you, everything alright?" Scary Pumpkin asked.

"Yes, we are fine, now let her go, our fight is not with her," I requested.

"You are the club leader," Scary Pumpkin released his grip on Ginger, she dropped to the ground. The boys walked over to Scary Pumpkin and Ginger.

"Hello, my name is Jerry, and these are my friends; Sammy and Ray-Ray," I introduced all of us.

"Hello boys, my name is Ginger, thanks for calling off the big guy," Ginger said.

"You are welcome, we only wish to travel through the Lost Woods, we mean no harm," I said to Ginger.

"May I ask, what are you guys up too?" Ginger inquired.

"We are on our way to see the Witch of the East," responded Scary Pumpkin.

"Oh really? Are you friends of hers?" Ginger asked.

"No way! We are going to kill her," said Ray-Ray.

"Are you and the rest of the Leopard Lizards friends of the Witch of the East," I asked.

"NO! After she destroyed our town, she changed me and my five sisters into what you see now," Ginger responded angrily and continued, "Please, it is not safe to talk about the Evil Witch here, come back to our hut, we know a way to get into the castle."

"That sounds great, let's go," I said to Ginger.

Ginger along with her sisters led the way back to their hut followed by my friends, Scary Pumpkin and I. As we all walked, I said, "I wonder where Ruby went?"

Back in Munchkin Land, The Captain along with a dozen flying monkeys were still high in the sky, "Hey, look down there, it is the Munchkin farmers pumpkin patch," shouted one of the flying monkeys.

"Good," replied the Captain, "Let's fly down and find our missing brother." He closed his wings and dived straight down followed by the dozen flying monkeys.

They circled the pumpkin field until the Captain spotted something, "Over here!" the Captain said.

He landed near a long pole in the center of the pumpkin patch; he was soon joined by the rest of the pack.

"This looks like the spot where a scarecrow was placed," said the Captain. He bent down and picked up the pole and its broken rope, "This must have been used to hold up the scarecrow."

"Hey, there is blood over here," spoke another flying monkey nearby.

The Captain and the rest of the pack walked over to see a large red spot along with a ripped-up uniform lying on the ground next to some pumpkins. There were parts of the Captain everywhere.

"What kind of monster could rip apart our brother?" One of the flying monkeys asked.

"I know what kind of monster that could do this." a tiny voice spoke from behind a pumpkin.

"Who said that?" The Captain asked.

"I did!" The Rat answered as he jumped on top a large pumpkin.

"Oh, really," the Captain said as he knelt to look at him.

"Yes! But it is going to cost you!" The rat replied.

"What is your price?" The Captain asked.

"Cheese! I want some cheese," the rat said.

"I don't have any cheese," answered the Captain, "Now tell me what I want to know!"

"I smell cheese, someone here has cheese on them, give me cheese!" The rat repeated.

The Captain looked at the dozen flying monkeys, "Everyone empty out your pockets."

Each one of the flying monkeys reached into their pockets and pulled out everything and set it on the ground in front of the Captain. The rat ran over to the pack of flying monkeys' things and smelled everything placed on the ground.

"Here! The cheese is there," pointed the rat at a wrapped piece of paper. The Captain walked over to it, picked it up and opened it.

"Oh look, it is a piece of cheesecake, will this do?" The Captain asked.

The rat jumped up and down with excitement, "Yes! Give it to me," he shouted.

"First, tell me what happened to our brother," demanded the Captain.

"Ok, I will tell you what happened here," spoke the rat, then he took a deep breath, "Your brother landed in the pumpkin patch near the Munchkins scarecrow, he poured something over its pumpkin head turning him into a monster, then your brother made the monster mad and the monster that was named, Scary Pumpkin by him, killed and ate him; then the Scary Pumpkin joined three Munchkin boys and a parrot and took off down the yellow brick road, that is the whole story! Now may I please have the cheese?" The Captain handed the cheese to the rat. The rat grabbed it and ran off to enjoy his reward.

The Captain looked at the flying monkey standing beside him, "Fly back to the castle and tell master what has happened here." The flying monkey jumped into the air and soon was on his way back to the castle to inform the Evil Witch. "Now, the rest of us will follow the yellow brick road and find Mr. Scary Pumpkin, three Munchkin boys and one parrot."

Ruby was still flying in the Northland and was now close to the castle of the Good Witch of the North, after she flew over a small mountain, the castle was in site, "There it is," she told herself, she circled the castle, she noticed an open window, she flew through it and down a long hallway into the main room of the castle and landed on a golden bird stand, "Hello, is anyone home," she shouted.

A Bear-Man came walking into the room, "Hello Ruby, it is great to see you again," he said as he walked over to her.

"It is nice to see you again Bob, can I speak with the Good Witch please?" Ruby asked.

"I am sorry, but she is not here," answered Bob.

"Where is she?" Ruby asked.

"The alarm bell rang in the Northern part of the land and she along with the Bear-Man army went there to help protect the town," Bob explained. Why do you ask? Is there anything wrong?" he continued.

Ruby looked at him, "Yes, Bob I think so, I think the Good Witch and the Bear-Man army were sent far away so the Evil Witches could attack on the opposite land."

"Well there is no way to contact her now," Bob answered disappointedly.

"Let me think," Ruby said.

Bob stood beside her and waited for her to speak again.

A little while later Ruby said, "Please tell the Good Witch to meet me at the border land of the East and North, near Munchkin town as soon as she gets back, I think both Evil Witches will attack there!"

"You can't fight both Evil Witches alone!" Bob remarked.

"Oh, I am not alone, I have three Munchkin boys and one oversized scarecrow that is now a monster named Scary Pumpkin!" Ruby told him.

Bob did not know what to say, he just looked at her. Ruby continued, "I must get back to my friends," she flapped her wings and took off flying back the same way, saying good-bye as she did.

Bob yelled, "GOODBYE RUBY! I will tell the Good Witch what you told me!" Bob observed her fly away and wondered if that would be the last time he would ever see her again. Ruby was soon flying faster than any bird could on her way back to help her friends.

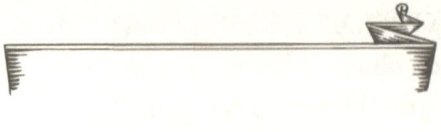

CHAPTER 10

LOST WOODS

MEANWHILE, DEEP IN the Lost Woods, the three of us boys, Scary Pumpkin, and the Leopard Lizards were still walking towards the hut.

"Are we almost there yet?" Ray-Ray asked.

"Just up the pathway a little more," replied Ginger, after a few more minutes she pointed, "There is our hut."

The Leopard Lizards hut was made from sticks and mud, it was round and about twenty feet in size, almost ten feet high and half was built below ground. Ginger reached the door first and knocked three times, the door slowly opened, and a Leopard Lizard stuck her head out to see who it was.

"It is Ginger, let me in." The door opened, Ginger walked in followed by four Leopard Lizards, three Munchkin boys and Scary Pumpkin who smiled at the Leopard Lizard holding the door open. She returned to the hut after being hurt in the fight earlier, she almost fell to the ground after seeing him.

"Please make yourself comfortable by the fire; I'll have some refreshments brought to you," Ginger said, she looked at two Leopard Lizards, "Please bring our first-time guest's refreshments."

They both went to another room while Ginger and the others sat down on skin rugs lying around the fireplace that was in the center of the hut. Once everyone was seated Ginger said, "I like to welcome you to our hut, we can talk freely here. We Leopard Lizards were cursed by the Witch of the East and forced to live in these woods and attack anything that comes in, she also turned us into what you see and out of the six of us, I am the only one that can speak, the Witch thought that would be funny, she along with her army of flying monkeys attacked our town and took everyone away to her dungeons, she only left us and put us here, the Lost Woods, we made our home here and wait for the day we can free our loved ones."

The two Leopard Lizards came back into the room carrying trays of drinks and homemade cookies, they walked over to us boys, we each took a cup and a couple of cookies but when they went over to Scary Pumpkin, he just shook his head no.

"Oh, don't mind him, he is still a little mad about the fight, he will be fine soon," I remarked to the two Leopard Lizards.

Now, can you tell us, how are you all going to get past all those flying monkeys, then kill the Witch of the East in her castle?" Ginger inquired.

"I would also like to hear that," spoke Scary Pumpkin.

"I will be happy to," I said, I stood up, "Our plan is simple, we go to the Witches castle, sneak in and steal her magic wand, sneak back out and back to our tree fort club, she will be so mad, she will chase us there, we can trap and kill her with water and fire."

Scary Pumpkin looked at me, Sammy, and Ray-Ray and said, "That is your plan?"

Ginger looked at Scary Pumpkin, he looked back at her, they both started to laugh and before long all three of us boys joined in along with the Leopard Lizards. I started to laugh along with everyone else while thinking to myself, "Why does everyone laugh at our plan?" After a few minutes of everyone laughing, Ginger stopped and looked at me.

"I am sorry to laugh at your plan, please forgive me," Ginger said.

"It is okay, we are getting use to a lot of people laughing at our plan," I replied.

"If you have a better plan, we would love to hear it," said Sammy.

Ginger looked at him, "Well, the fact of the matter is, we do!" Everyone stopped laughing.

"You do? What is it?" Ray-Ray asked.

.

Ginger looked at a Leopard Lizard and said, "Go get the map." The Leopard Lizard left the room and quickly returned carrying a rolled-up map and gave it to Ginger who unrolled the map on the ground in front of us boys, all of us looked at it while Ginger explained it to them, "This map was made many years ago, it was left at our door by someone with a note saying, 'Give this map to the brave ones.'"

We looked at Ginger saying, "We are not brave, believe me!"

Anyone that is going to the Witch's castle is brave; this map must be for you. "Now, let's get to it," Ginger said, "We are here, the map shows a short cut to the border land and a secret tunnel that goes under the castle and comes out inside the dungeons of the castle. Once inside, we open all the cell doors releasing the prisoners. After they are set free, they will attack the Witch and her flying monkeys from the inside and hopefully one of them will kill that Witch in the prison riot that is going to happen."

I looked at Ginger and said, "Why do you say, once we get into the castle?"

"We are going with you, that is why," Ginger answered, "The Witch will find out we helped you and when she does, she will kill us and our loved ones in the dungeons."

I looked at Sammy and Ray-Ray, then Scary Pumpkin, "Well guys, it looks like our club is now going to have six more new members, if it is okay with all of you."

The boys and Scary Pumpkin smiled, "Welcome to the Lollipop Kids Club!"

"Now, we are eleven strong," Sammy said excitedly.

Ginger looked at him puzzled, "I only count ten of us,"

"There is one more member of our club, she took off somewhere, but I am sure she will rejoin us soon," I remarked.

"What is a lollipop?" Ginger asked.

I reached into my pants pocket and pulled out a handful of lollipops, handed Ginger one along with the rest of the Leopard Lizards, "These are lollipops, I make them myself," he also gave one to Sammy, Ray-Ray, and Scary Pumpkin, soon everyone was taking a lollipop break.

After they finished eating the lollipops, Ginger said, "Taste good! Now you all finish your drinks and snacks, let us get out of here and follow that short cut on the map."

I said, "We are ready." I rolled up the map and put it in my backpack. Sammy and Ray-Ray stood up along with Scary Pumpkin.

The hut door opened, and Ginger said, "Three of you go ahead of us to make sure everything is clear, we will meet you at the border land." Three Leopard Lizards started to run toward the border while the boys rode on the backs of the remaining three Leopard Lizards and Scary Pumpkin walked fast behind them towards the Witches castle.

Not so far away, back inside the castle of the Witch of the East, The Witch of the West looked at her sister, "I waited long enough, the sun will be setting soon, let's fly out with our armies and find out what is going on ourselves."

"Yes, I agree, something has gone wrong," answered the Witch of the East to her older, wiser sister. Both sisters stood up, put down their mugs of witches' brew and picked up their brooms. It was not long before the two Evil Witches made their way down the hallway and up the stairway to the roof top where hundreds of flying monkeys were waiting for their evil Masters. The two Witches climbed up onto a landing platform in the center of the castle roof.

"Tonight is Hallow Eve night; we are going into battle against the Good Witch of the South and maybe the North too!" The Witch of the West announced. The two armies cheered.

Now, let us unite as one and destroy those Good Witches, and the three Munchkins," announced the Witch of the East, then she raised her broom in the air, "Let's fly." Both witches sat on their brooms.

"Off to the forbidden zone land," they both said together. The brooms shot into the sunset, the sounds of the two Evil Witches laughing and hundreds of flying monkeys' wings filled the air.

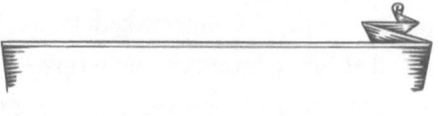

CHAPTER 11

FORBIDDEN ZONE

AFTER SOME TIME OF following the short cut through the rest of the Lost Woods, Ginger said, "We are coming to the end of the woods, just ahead is the border land between this side of Good and when you cross over to the other side you will be in the land of Evil, home of the Witch of the East."

As they walked out into the wide-open field, they were met by the three Leopard Lizards that Ginger ordered to scout ahead. The three of us climbed off the Leopard Lizards and stood beside them. The group of ten now looked at the open field, and the other side. It was dead looking; no signs of life or any kind of sound could be heard.

Scary Pumpkin looked at the evil land, grinning said, "So that is the land of an Evil Witch? I like the look of it."

Ginger looked up at him, "You would!"

"I sure wish Ruby would get back," said Ray-Ray.

"Me too! Sammy replied.

"Who is Ruby," Ginger asked.

"Oh, she is our very first club member, she joined us this morning." Sammy said excitedly.

"Yea, she is a special kind of parrot with magic powers," said Ray-Ray.

"So, what happened to her?" Ginger asked.

We all just looked at Scary Pumpkin, he returned their looks, "Go ahead, tell her, it will give you something to talk about while we cross to the other side." He then started to walk straight ahead, across the open field.

I said, "We better follow the big guy while I tell you about Ruby." I started walking and began the story as the group marched in line behind Scary Pumpkin. "Well, earlier today as we were walking, Ruby was sitting on the big guy's shoulder, and something came up and she flew off."

"What came up?" Ginger questioned.

"You should have said, something came out!" Sammy remarked. Ray-Ray started to laugh and so did I.

SCARY PUMPKIN TURNED his head around, "That is a good one!" and began laughing.

I looked at Ginger, "He passed a lot of gas that made Ruby GO! GO!"

Ginger and the rest of the Leopard Lizards joined in with the laughter, not knowing of the danger flying high above them. The two Evil Witches were flying high as the sun set and the moon was starting to rise.

The Witch of the West said, "Sister, why don't you fly ahead, take half of the army with you, when you see the Munchkins or Good Witches make sure they are in the border land, then start your attack. When the Good Witches appear, I will make sure to cut them off and we will fight them without the safety of the Good land to shield them, their power will be limited, while ours will only grow as the moon rises on this Hallow Eve."

"Okay, sister, that sounds like a fun plan," remarked the Witch of the East, "But remember, I want my fight to be with the Good Witch of the South, you take her sister, the Good Witch of the North."

The Witch of the West smiled at her sister and reached over to shake her hand, "It is a deal."

They both smiled at each other and shook hands. "Now, I will fly down below with the rest of the army and wait until you send me a sign that the Good Witch is there." She then waved good-bye to her sister and flew to the ground below along with over a hundred flying monkeys. When they landed on the ground, the Witch of the West said to her army, "Everyone take cover, until I call you." Within minutes they were hidden out of site, only she stood holding her broom waiting for her sister to call. The Witch of the East along with over a hundred flying monkeys kept flying towards the forbidden zone and the land of the Good Witch of the South.

Our Lollipop Club was halfway across the open field when Sammy pointed at the moon, "Hey, look at how fast the moon is rising." They all stopped and looked at the moon.

"Hey, it is starting to change colors too," remarked RayRay.

"It is turning my favorite color, blood red," said Scary Pumpkin, then he turned his pumpkin head around, "We are being followed." The Leopard Lizards quickly knelt and got ready for an attack, while us boys reached into our backpacks and pulled out our weapons.

I looked across the field to the other side, "Let's get out of here, we are sitting ducks."

Ginger said, "You boys get on our backs fast, we will carry you the rest of the way." I jumped on Ginger's back while Sammy and Ray-Ray climbed on two other Leopard Lizards. Ginger started to run with me holding on, Sammy and Ray-Ray were close behind holding on to the two Leopard Lizards and three more were running up beside them.

Scary Pumpkin said, "I will meet you all on the other side." He did not fear anything, he just took big steps following the running

Leopard Lizards towards the land of evil. The one flying monkey that was ordered to report back to the Witch was still flying high in the sky when he saw the Witch flying on her broom, just behind her, the early night sky was filled with flying monkeys. He flew towards the witch and soon reached her.

"STOP!" The flying monkey told the Witch of the East. The Witches broom froze in midair, while the flying monkeys stayed in place flapping its wings. "Master, I bring news," he said, then told her all he knew. The Captain getting killed, the Scarecrow monster that is now working with the Munchkins and about the parrot named Ruby.

"WHAT! That scarecrow will pay double for crossing me," replied the Witch of the East in a bitter tone. "Where are they now," she demanded to know.

"We believe they are heading this way and should be at the border land now," the flying monkey told her, "The Captain sent me to relay this message to you while he and the rest of the pack followed their tracks and will be ready when you need them."

"Good!" The Witch answered, "You may fly back to the castle and rest while I go pay back that scarecrow and a few more little things."

"Yes master," the flying monkey responded. He flew past his fellow brothers.

"Fly ahead and keep your eyes open for those Munchkins and their friends, they must be nearby," the Witch demanded. The broom took off again, it lowered just over the top of a tall dead forest that was just below the Witches Mountain. Scary Pumpkin suddenly stopped walking and looked behind him, out from the Lost Woods a dozen mad looking flying monkeys came walking out. They looked at him and slowly walked towards him, Scary Pumpkin just stood there and smiled, waiting for them.

I turned and saw where Scary Pumpkin was, "STOP!" I yelled. Ginger stopped fast along with the rest of the Leopard Lizards. "Turn around fast, one of our club members is in trouble!!" I told them with urgency.

CHAPTER 12

LOLLIPOP KID CLUB DOES BATTLE

THE LEOPARD LIZARDS saw Scary Pumpkin and the flying monkeys getting ready to attack. "Let's go help the big guy!" Ginger said as she started running as fast as she could towards Scary Pumpkin, the rest of the Leopard Lizards were close behind, the boys were cheering and getting their weapons ready to fire.

Scary Pumpkin heard Ginger and looked at her coming towards him, "STOP!! GO BACK!! I do not need any help; there are only a dozen of them." He yelled.

Ginger stopped, "Well, you heard him."

"We will just wait here until he is done," I said.

"Oh no, look up at the moon and all those flying monkeys coming this way," said Ray-Ray.

"It is the Witch of the East and her army," stated Sammy.

"Hey, Scary Pumpkin get over here, we need your help!" I shouted.

Scary Pumpkin turned away from the dozen flying monkeys slowly coming at him, "Okay, I am coming," he then started walking fast towards me and the rest of the Lollipop Kids Club members.

"Look down below in the middle of the forbidden zone, it is those Munchkins, Leopard Lizards and that monster you made," spoke the flying monkey flying next to the Evil Witch.

"Broom take me down there to those Munchkin boys," said the Witch of the East.

"Here comes the Witch and her army, everyone make a circle and we will fight them together," I ordered.

Scary Pumpkin reached the group and joined them in making a circle; each member had their weapon out and was ready for the Witches attack. I waited until the first wave of flying monkeys came into range, when they did, I shouted, "FIRE!"

We all shot our weapons at the oncoming flying monkeys, each shot hit a flying monkey knocking them out, and they fell to the ground below. Scary Pumpkin jumped high in the air and caught the flying monkeys by their tails, they screamed as Scary Pumpkin pulled them back to the ground. The two flying monkeys tried to fight him off, but it was no use, the Witches spell made him stronger than a dozen of the flying monkeys.

It only took a moment for the two flying monkeys to meet their end; Scary Pumpkin dropped their dead bodies to the ground and looked up trying to find the Witch of the East. A group of six flying monkeys hit Scary Pumpkin at the same time knocking him off his feet to the ground. Ginger and the rest of the Leopard Lizards were great fighters; they have been fighting for over a hundred years in the Witches woods.

Ginger shouted, "OKAY GIRLS, IT'S TIME TO USE OUR SECRET WEAPONS." The boys looked at Ginger and the five Leopard Lizards and wondered what she was talking about. Flying monkeys were now landing by the dozens around them; the dozen flying monkeys that were tracking them now joined up with the rest of the Witches army blocking the way back to the good land of the South. Ginger started to run at a group of flying monkeys swinging wooden clubs in the air. The rest of the Leopard Lizards ran on both sides of her protecting Ginger from any attacks from the sides or behind. Just as the Leopard Lizards were getting close to the flying monkeys, Ginger just disappeared, then the rest of the Leopard Lizards did the same thing, they were all gone.

"Hey, where did those Leopard Lizards go?" One of the flying monkeys asked.

Suddenly, he and the other flying monkeys were hit by the invisible tails of the Leopard Lizards, after they knocked out those flying monkeys then they went after more. The flying monkeys tried to hit them by swinging their wooden clubs, but they could not see them and only hit themselves and other flying monkeys, soon fights started to break out between the flying monkeys. The Witch of the East was sitting on her broom flying over the fighting below.

"I still don't see the Good Witches, but I do see a scarecrow with a pumpkin head and six Leopard Lizards that double crossed me!" The Witch of the East said aloud to herself.

Scary Pumpkin stood up and threw off the flying monkeys attacking him like they were toys. Then he looked up and saw the Witch.

"There you are master!" Scary Pumpkin shouted.

The Evil Witch looked at him, "It is time you meet your maker," She answered.

Scary Pumpkin looked at the boys still firing their weapons, "It has been fun being one of the Lollipop Kids Club members, he bent down then leapt towards the witch, he was flying straight at her when two flying monkeys flew in front of him, Scary Pumpkin reached out his long arms and stuck out his claws and ripped them both in half with one swing of his hand, it didn't slow him down, he was still flying towards the witch.

The Witch gave him an evil grin, aimed her broom at him, "BROOM," she yelled out, "FIRE ONE FIREBALL!" Scary Pumpkin's eyes popped wide open as he saw a cannon ball size fireball coming straight at his pumpkin head.

"NO!" We yelled together as we saw Scary Pumpkins' head get blown apart, the fireball lit up the battlefield, then like snowflakes, hot sticky pumpkin seeds started to fall from the sky. When the seeds touched something, they stuck to it like glue.

CHAPTER 13

GOOD AND EVIL WITCHES BATTLE

I TOLD MY FRIENDS TO give up the fight after seeing Scary Pumpkin get blown up and lay their weapons down, the flying monkeys grabbed us and held the three of us prisoners. The Leopard Lizards were still fighting when the sticky pumpkin seeds started to hit and stick to them, exposing them to everyone.

The Witch laughed and shouted, "Peek-a-Boo, we can all see you!"

"Oh no, the pumpkin seeds will make us visible," Ginger yelled out. The flying monkeys now could see the Leopard Lizards because of the seeds sticking on them and smiled, in minutes dozens of flying monkeys were attacking the Leopard Lizards and they also had no choice but to surrender. The Evil Witch of the East landed her broom near the three Munchkin boys and the Leopard Lizards now being held prisoners and looked each one in the eyes.

"So, which one of you, is called Jerry?" The Evil Witch asked.

The boys and Leopard Lizards looked at each other and smiled, they all took a step toward the Witch, "I am Jerry," they all said together. The flying monkeys started to laugh after seeing and hearing the prisoners.

The Witch grinned, and then walked in front of me, "So, you are the leader of the Lollipop Kids Club, and you want to kill me?" I said nothing. Sammy, Ray-Ray, and I just kept our heads low.

"Oh, leave them alone you ugly looking witch!" Ginger stated loudly.

The Witch stood up, walked over to Ginger who was held down by five flying monkeys, her sisters were still knocked out from the battle. "Now, Ginger, didn't I warn you against disobeying me? After, I emptied that town of yours so many years ago."

"One day you are going to pay for what you did to our town folks, my sisters and I," replied Ginger angrily.

The Witch laughed while pulling her magic wand from inside her cape pocket. Ginger knew she only had a minute or two; she looked at her sister, "Take care!"

The Witch touched Ginger's forehead with her wand, "May you live forever as a statue from inside my castle." The tip of the wand flashed a bright light and Ginger was instantly turned into a stone statue. There was still the remaining five Leopard Lizards which the Witch pointed at them, "Take them to my dungeons; I will deal with them later."

"Yes master!" A group of flying monkeys standing guard over a knocked-out brother responded. Four of the flying monkeys picked up one Leopard Lizard and started to fly up into the moon light back to the castle of the East. It took over a dozen flying monkeys to pick up the rest of the Leopard Lizards and fly them back to the castle.

The Witch turned to face the boys, "Now it is your turn," she raised her magic wand at them and was getting ready to cast a spell when a beam of red light hit her. The beam knocked the Witch off her feet backwards yards away; it also broke her broom. The flying monkeys that were holding the boy's prisoners released them and slowly backed up after seeing the Witch get knocked out cold. The boys smiled as soon as they saw where the red beam of light came from.

"IT IS RUBY!" I shouted. We all cheered together as they watched her fly towards them, she landed on a dead tree stump next to us.

"Sorry it took me so long, I see you all found the Witch of the East," teased Ruby. We all walked over to her, when we were near her, she said, "It is time I show my true appearance," Ruby reached up and took off the tiny pair of ruby colored shoes and laid them on the ground, then she stepped into them, the parrot changed into the most beautiful Witch of the South.

"WOW! All the boys remarked together after seeing her standing in front of them. The Good Witch of the South was tall with long wavy red hair; she was wearing a body outfit that fit like a glove.

"We knew that you were not a real parrot," remarked Ray-Ray. The boys gave her a hug.

"Thanks for joining our club and watching out for us," I remarked.

"Oh, you are welcome," she answered.

"I can't believe you killed the Witch of the East so easily," said Sammy.

Ruby looked at the boys and whispered so the nearby flying monkeys could not hear, "Boys I didn't kill the Witch only knocked her out for a few minutes but don't tell the flying monkeys that."

"What! She is still alive?" I asked.

"Yes, so listen to what I am about to tell you," Ruby said to them, "I can only stay on this land for a short time before I lose my power and become helpless." Ruby took my hand, "Walk with me, I have something to give you for your birthday." Sammy and Ray-Ray walked over to Ginger and looked at her while the two talked. "Jerry, you are a very special boy, I want to give you a birthday gift," the Good Witch of the South smiled, she took out her magic wand, touched my head, "My gift to you can only be used and granted on the Munchkins homeland. I grant you a birthday wish." The star on the tip of her wand lit up, my entire body shook, then it stopped.

"What just happened?" I asked, but before Ruby could answer, she was hit by a lightning bolt from the tip of the Witch of the East's wand.

"That is for breaking my favorite broom," cried out the Witch of the East. Ruby was the one hurt now, she was thrown to the ground and not moving. I was knocked down also because I was standing close to her. I slowly stood up and went over to Ruby's side to check on her. The Witch of the East slowly walked towards me and Ruby, her flying monkeys were cheering seeing their master alive and the Good Witch knocked out or dead.

"Please, wake up Ruby, the Evil Witch is coming," I cried out to her as I shook her.

Ruby slowly opened her eyes, "Help me up." I smiled at her, helped her back up to face the Evil Witch, she stopped when she saw Ruby stand back up. "It is going to take more than one lightning bolt to keep me down," remarked Ruby.

"Ok with me, have another one!" The Evil Witch replied. The Evil Witch pointed her magic wand at Ruby again, but this time Ruby was ready, she pulled her magic wand out and it changed into a large umbrella with hundreds of tiny mirrors placed on the outside of it. Another lightning bolt and it deflected back towards the Witch of the East who quickly dove out of the way just in time causing the group of flying monkeys standing behind her to be hit and caught on fire. They started to roll around on the ground to put themselves out.

The Evil Witch picked herself up off the ground, looked at Ruby "That was a good one," she remarked as she dusted herself off.

"Thanks, I am glad you liked it," answered Ruby sarcastically.

"I can tell by those shoes that your power is almost up," stated the Evil Witch. I looked down at Ruby's shoes, they were fading in color. Ruby lowered the umbrella as she did it changed back to her magic wand.

"Are you okay, Ruby?" I asked her in a concern tone.

"Just remember what I told you," she responded, "Now, please move away from me so we Witches can finish our fight." I did as Ruby asked, I walked over to where Sammy, Ray-Ray and the statue of Ginger were.

The Evil Witch started to walk closer to Ruby, "I don't think you can take another hit from my wand, if you get up now and give me your shoes, I will spare the life of the three Munchkin boys and you!"

"If I give up my shoes your powers will grow, I will never give evil more power," Ruby stated.

"Have it your way," replied the Evil Witch, she quickly pointed her wand at Ruby again, "Take this!" Another lightning bolt shot out from her wand, Ruby raised her wand again but this time her wand did not change, and Ruby was hit. The lightning bold hit her hard, knocking her backward to the ground, she was helpless as the Evil Witch started to walk towards her. The boys started to run to her, but they were grabbed by flying monkeys and held in place. "Tonight, you die," the Witch said as she pointed her wand at Ruby for the final strike, suddenly a loud noise came from the Witches woods. The Evil Witch turned to look at what the noise was, Ruby also looked and smiled when she saw what the noise was.

"IT IS MY SISTER, GLINDA and the army of Bear-Man." The Evil Witch slowly backed up to her army of flying monkeys after seeing the Good Witch of the North and her army of Bear-Man. Ruby slowly stood up and shouted to Glinda, "Stay where you are, it's a trap!" Ruby told her.

The Good Witch of the North stopped at the edge of the Lost Woods along with over a hundred Bear-Man.

"Sister, what are you doing over there?" Glinda asked.

"Sister, quick send over your Bear-Man army, we need help," Ruby replied.

Glinda looked at her Captain of the Bear-Man, "GO!! Attack those flying monkeys and that Evil Witch!"

The Captain looked at the Bear-Man and roared, "CHARGE!" He started to run into the open field of the borderland towards Ruby and the Munchkin boys, over a hundred Bear-Man were close behind him with their mouths wide open showing off their large teeth.

CHAPTER 14

HALLOW EVE,
EVIL WITCHES NIGHT

THE EVIL WITCH OF THE East looked at her army of flying monkeys, "Attack those Bear-Man!" Flying monkeys jumped into the air carrying and swinging their wooden clubs. The two armies crashed together in the open field. The flying monkeys knew the Bear-Man were bigger and stronger, so they attacked them from the air. The Bearman were taking blows to their heads and becoming angrier as they were trying to jump up and grab them, but the flying monkeys knew just how high they could jump and were able to stay out of their reach.

After some time, fighting, Glinda shouted, "FORGET THE FLYING MONKEYS, SAVE MY SISTER AND THE BOYS!" The Bear-Man army gave up on the flying monkeys and started to run towards the Witch of the East still standing watch with a small group of flying monkeys.

"I guess it is time for some help," the Witch of the East remarked as she pointed her wand toward the night sky, the wand fired three bright fire balls straight up into the air. I, Sammy, and Ray-Ray watched the fire balls shoot into the sky.

"Why did that witch do that?" Sammy asked.

"I don't know but I bet we are going to find out very soon," I replied. Not far away the Wicked Witch of the West was watching the full moon when she saw the three bright fire balls, "That is my sister's signal!" she shouted, she grabbed her broom and let out, "WE FLY NOW!" The broom took off towards the fire balls along with hundreds of flying monkeys.

The flying monkeys tried to stop the running Bear-Man, but they were too big, they were there when the Good Witch of the North yelled, "RUBY LOOK OUT!"

The boys also saw what was coming and shouted, "RUBY, TURN AROUND!!"

Ruby turned around and saw the Witch of the West flying on her broom coming straight at her. The Witch kicked Ruby as she flew by on her broom. Ruby fell backwards again and hit the ground.

"I will take care of the Good Witch of the North and the Bear-Man, finish off the Good Witch of the South!" The Witch of the West said to her sister, as her along with hundreds of flying monkeys flew at the oncoming Bear-Man. Glinda was still sitting on her white unicorn watching the battle, she wanted to join the fight, but she knew better than going into that field and lose her power. The Witch of the West pointed her wand and waved it at some rocks in front of the Bear-Man, "I want you rocks to come alive, grow and block those Bear-man from helping the Good Witch." With fascination the rocks started to grow until they were extremely bigger than the Bear-Man. The rocks came alive and stood in a line blocking the way to Ruby.

The Witch of the West then ordered her flying monkeys to join in the fight with the Bear-Man as she flew forward.

Glinda was on the edge of the Lost Woods. "Well, hello there Glinda, it has been a long time." The Witch of the West cackled.

"Not long enough," answered the Good Witch of the North. Both Witches pointed their wands at each other as they talked.

"You can't save your sister, her power is almost gone now, and our power is glowing at the full moon on this night of Hallow Eve," remarked the Evil Witch of the West.

Glinda knew she was right, if she crossed into that field, she would soon lose her powers, if that happened, both Evil Witches would take over the lands of the East, West, North and South. Both Witches kept an eye on each other while also watching the battle going on.

The Witch of the East picked up one half of her broken broom and slowly walked towards Ruby helplessly laying on the ground, her power almost gone, her ruby shoes now turning black.

"LEAVE HER ALONE!" I cried out, still being held along with Sammy and Ray-Ray by flying monkeys.

The Witch stopped and looked at the boys and smiled, "Don't worry about her, after I kill her, you boys are next!"

The Bear-Man army hit the Rock Man blocking their way, but they just bounced off, they tried to climb over them, but the Rock Man used their long rock arms and hands to throw them off and backwards. The Witch of the West laughed as she watched the Bear-Man being stopped and now being attacked by more flying monkeys. Glinda watched, she knew the Witch of the West was just waiting for her to try something, so she could be trapped, like her sister was now, so she stayed sitting on her unicorn hoping that her sister could somehow get away.

Ruby now laying on the ground looked over at her sister, "My power is gone sister, please protect my beloved Munchkins for me," then she looked at the three boys, smiled at them, "Thanks for the adventure my friends, I am sure your plan will work, then she gave them a wink."

The Witch of the East looked down at Ruby, "Have you any last words my dear?"

Ruby looked at her, "Yes, I do, you and that sister of yours may have won this battle but good will overcome evil in the end."

"Is that all you have to say?" The Evil Witch remarked.

"One more thing," said Ruby, "I hope sometime soon a house falls from the clear blue sky and lands on top of that pointed hat of yours!"

The Witch laughed at her response then raised half of her broken broom and stabbed Ruby in the heart.

"NO" Cried out the Good Witch of the North as she saw her sister get stabbed and killed. The boys also screamed as they saw Ruby die in front of them, tears rolled down their faces along with Glinda's. The Bear-Man army stopped the fight and roared in pain when they saw the Good Witch of the South was now dead and they failed to save her. They slowly retreated to the Good Witch of the North to protect her.

The Witch of the West saw the Bear-Man coming back so she said, "Broom lift me up out of reach of the Bearman." The broom rose up high enough to keep the Witch safe. The Good Witch of the North was still in shock after seeing her sister killed, for the first time in her long life she did not know what to do. She just stared at Ruby's dead body lying on the ground.

The Captain of the Bear-Man returned to her, "I am sorry, we failed you my Good Witch, we tried to reach the Good Witch of the South but those Evil Witches magic was to strong, we better retreat back to the castle and prepare for another attack from them."

The Witch of the East reached down and pulled Ruby's now black shoes off her, then she took off her long black boots and put on the pair of shoes. They started to glow and change color until they returned to a Ruby color. The Witch smiled, "I can feel the power from my new shoes." She then picked up both halves of her broken broom and raised them into the air, "Broom come back together again." Her new shoes started to glow again, and her broom snapped back together better than before. The Witch sat on it, "Broom take me to my sister." The broom shot off into the air and soon was flying beside the Witch of the West. Now both Witches were facing Glinda with their magic wand out and pointed at her.

Glinda looked at them, "You win the battle tonight and you killed my only sister, now you have the right to rule the land she once protected. I will return to my castle with my Bear-Man army. I would like to have my sister's body to take back with me."

Both Evil Witches looked at each other than the Witch of the West said, "We will give you one night to mourn the loss of your sister, then our battle will be with you! We will let two of the Munchkin boys bring her body to you, but one will remain with us to make sure that all the Munchkins will keep on picking the food for our flying monkeys."

Glinda looked at both witches and nodded her head showing she understood. Both Evil Witches turned away from Glinda and the Bear-Man army and flew back to where the Munchkin boys were still being held.

They landed near the boys saying, "Thank you boys for helping us kill one of the Good Witches." My friends and I were still crying about Ruby's murder and the words of the Evil Witches only made us feel worse. "Now, two of you take your friends body back across the field to Glinda while one of you will come back to my castle to be my guest," said the Witch of the East. We all looked at each other wondering who was going back home and who was going back to the castle of the Witch of the East.

"Who is the leader of this brave little group?" The Witch of the West asked them.

I took one step forward, "I am the club leader," I said while wiping the tears from my eyes.

"So, you will be going with us while your two friends will be going back home, say goodbye to each other," said the Witch of the West.

I looked at my two friends, "Take care my friends, don't worry about me, I will be okay."

Sammy and Ray-Ray gave me a hug and when they did, I whispered, "Do not worry, our plan may have changed but it still could work. I will break out somehow and see both of you at our tree fort." Sammy and Ray-Ray gave him a puzzled look but said nothing.

"Release the two boys," ordered the Witch of the East to the flying monkeys holding Sammy and Ray-Ray.

The Witch of the West pointed her magic wand at Ruby's body, "Give me a sled with wheels and put her body on it." Ruby's body lifted a few feet and a sled with wheels and ropes attached to it appeared, Ruby's body lowered onto it. "Now you two boys take the Good dead Witch with you back to her sister and make sure you tell everyone back in Munchkin land not to ever disobey us again. If they do, next time we will not be so nice! Now go, before we change our minds," the Witch of the West warned.

Sammy and Ray-Ray walked over to Ruby's body lying on the sled, they each picked up one rope that was tied to it and started pulling it back across the open field to where the Good Witch of the North was waiting along with her Bear-Man army.

I watched my friends pull the Good Witch of the South away and thought to myself, "It is my fault she is dead," I then looked over to Ginger's statue, "I'll free you somehow."

"I don't think so," laughed the Witch of the East, "We will talk more once we get back to my castle, now take him and the statue of our friend Ginger back to the castle," ordered the Witch of the East.

One flying monkey grabbed my arms and jumped into the air, it took four flying monkeys to lift Ginger, soon all the Witches new prisoners were flying high in the moonlit sky back to the castle.

I could only watch as I was taken away, I could see below Sammy and Ray-Ray pulling the sled, Glinda on her unicorn with her Bear-Man army all around her. "Boy, how did I ever get into a mess like this?" I said aloud to myself.

The flying monkey overheard my comment and started to laugh, "Just lucky, I guess." He said.

Both of the Evil sisters watched the boys as they left and once, they were out of sight the Witch of the East asked her sister, "Now that they cannot hear us, tell me why we did not kill Glinda back there?

The Witch of the West smiled, "Because my sister, I need that magic wand of hers and that must be handled in a most delicate way. You have those nice Ruby shoes and all the power it comes with; well, the same thing will happen when I kill her and get that wand of hers."

"Oh, I understand now, so how and when do we do that?" The Witch of the East asked her sister.

"I need to check out some writing in the book of spells, I will fly back to my castle and do some reading, I will meet you back at your castle before dawn with the answer to that question, my dear sister. So, take my army with you and start celebrating the death of the Good Witch of the South," the Witch of the West sat on her broom and laughed, "Broom back home!" She took off flying, her laughter could be heard until she was out of sight.

THE WITCH OF THE EAST watched her fly away and laughed, then she looked over at two hundred flying monkeys,

"Let's all go back to my place for a party!"

The flying monkeys cheered and shouted, "PARTY! PARTY!"

The Witch grabbed her broom and looked once more at her new Ruby shoes and smiled, "LET'S FLY!" The Witch shouted; her broom took off into the moon lit night.

The flying monkeys quickly jumped into the air after her still shouting, "PARTY! PARTY!"

CHAPTER 15

THE WITCHES DUNGEON

SAMMY AND RAY-RAY REACHED across the field, Glinda watched the last of the Evil Witches and both armies of flying monkeys fly away and then saw the boys pulling her sister's body. "General, go get my sister's body, take it back to my castle, I will meet you there shortly," Glinda said somberly.

"As you wish," the General responded, and then he went over to Sammy and Ray-Ray, "Thanks boys, I will take her from here." The boys dropped the rope and the General picked up Ruby's body and carried her in his large arms and started to head towards the castle.

"Follow him, make sure nothing happens to my sister's body," Glinda told the rest of the Bear-Man army. The Bear-Man did as they were ordered and followed behind the General back to the castle. The boys walked over to Glinda bowing their heads low in sadness. "Boys, I know you are sad, just like me, but Ruby wanted to help you boys and so do I. Now climb up and I will take you back to Munchkin Land," Glinda said.

The boys looked at Glinda, "We must save Jerry!" They said together.

"I am sure Jerry will find his way out, he is going to have a lot of friends when he gets there," Glinda replied.

"What do you mean?" Ray-Ray inquired of her.

"Her dungeons are filled with hundreds of prisoners that are good and they will help him and also each other if it all goes according to plan." Glinda told him, "Now get on, I will tell you what my sister planned while we head to safety behind the walls of the town." Sammy and Ray-Ray nodded their heads. Glinda reached down and took Sammy's hand pulling him up in front of her then reached down and grabbed Ray-Ray's hand and pulled him up behind her. "Now, hang on boys, we must fly!" Glinda told them. The Unicorn started to run and soon jumped into the air, large wings opened and quickly lifted the group of three high into the air over the Lost Woods back to Munchkin Land.

It was not a long flight back to the Evil Witches Castle and I could now see it from the air as we got closer to it. The flying monkey lowered his wings and landed on the landing platform along with the rest of the flying monkeys that were carrying six Leopard Lizards. The pack leader walked over to me, "Wait here, master will be coming soon." The flying monkey walked off the platform and left me, the knocked-out Leopard Lizards, and the statue of Ginger.

I walked over to the Leopard Lizards, and reached down and pleaded with them to wake up as I shook one of them, but it was no use, she just would not wake up. I stood up and looked around, then I heard sounds coming from the night sky above. Hundreds of flying monkeys were landing all over the castle, as they landed each one looked at me like I was soon to be dinner.

The Witch of the East landed her broom on the landing platform and looked at both flying monkey armies, "Welcome, well done to all of you for your part of helping me kill one of our beloved enemies, The Good Witch of the South.

The flying monkeys chanted, "Jerry! Jerry!

The Witch put up her hand, every flying monkey became quiet. "So, what should I do about you?" The Witch said loud enough for all the flying monkeys to hear.

A voice cried out from the crowd, "Let him spin the Witches wheel!"

The Witch smiled, "Good idea! Bring me the Witches wheel." The Witch looked at me, "You are going to play a game called; Witches wheel, to play this you can only spin the wheel once and whatever the pointer lands on that becomes your fate." Two big doors opened from one of the watch towers and out came a group of flying monkeys pushing a large wooden wheel on a cart. Once they reached the platform, they lifted it up and set it up on a stand in front of us. It stood almost ten feet tall and on side was a picture of a circle divided into pie shapes, Witch words were written inside them.

I looked at the words written on the wheel, and they said things like; cook me now, bake me into a pie and more funny and deadly things. After reading all my choices I asked, "How come I don't see any words saying, let him go or Kick the Evil Witch as hard as you can?"

"I will make note of that next time," the Witch replied to his comment, "Now spin the wheel, and let's see what is going to be your fate."

I walked up to the wheel, I looked up at it and grabbed the wheel, and I pulled down as hard as I could and then stepped back beside the Evil Witch. We both watched the wheel spin round and round until it slowed and stopped. The Witch looked at the pointer, "Well it looks like you are going to be our guest for a while."

I looked and read, "25 years in the deepest darkest dungeon cell."

"Sorry for your luck my boy, see you in 25 years, now don't be late." The Witch said laughing. Two flying monkeys picked me up and they made their way into the castle, down to the dungeons that had many levels. I did not say another word while being carried off to the dungeon below. The Witch now turned her attention back to the flying monkeys, "Now, let's get this party started," she waved her wand near her, "Give me a band, food and drinks." The platforms filled with mist and flashes of light started coming from inside. Soon the mist disappeared, and a band and many tables filled with every kind of food and drink a flying monkey would love appeared. Two more flying monkeys carried her favorite chair over to her; she sat down, "Let's hear some music." The band started to play one of the Witches favorite songs and the party was started.

I was now inside the fire lit stairway being led by two flying monkeys, "How far down does the steps go?" I inquired.

"All the way to the end, seven levels and that is where your new home is going to be," both flying monkeys laughed as they walked further down the stairway. After a few more levels they reached the end of the stairway, "This is your level Jerry, open the door and start walking down the hallway," the flying monkeys told me. I did as I was told and walked down the long hallway filled with cells of all kinds of prisoners from different lands that the Witch put there. As I walked by, I looked inside the cells and every prisoner looked at me smiling like they knew I was coming and were glad to see me. We soon reached the end of the hallway at the last cell on the deepest level of the dungeons. I stopped in front of the cell and looked in, an exceptionally large human-like man stood at the cell door; he was over three hundred pounds and had long arms and small legs that could not hold him up for long. "We have a new roommate for you Fat Albert," one of the flying monkeys said to the human-like man. The other one pushed on a button that was near a speaker box mounted to the cell door. Open cell door, level seven, cell one!"

"Will do," said a voice from the speaker. The cell door popped open, and I was pushed inside, and I stood in front of my new roommate.

"Now, you two be nice, we will be back to feed you breakfast in a few hours," said the flying monkeys laughing as they closed the cell door. "Now let's get back to the party," the other flying monkey said, they both ran back down the hallway and were soon out of sight.

"Hello Jerry, like you heard from those flying monkeys, my nickname is Fat Albert, it is nice to finally meet you. Some of us have been waiting a long time for this day to come," Fat Albert told me.

"Oh, really," I replied with a puzzled look on my face.

"Let me sit down, the Witch turned me this fat and with small legs, she thinks it is funny to watch me run and walk," Fat Albert explained. He then sat down on the bottom bunk. Next to the bunk was a small table with a bucket of water and a cup, there was a small hole in the ground that was used for the prisoner to relieve themselves and one small chair just the right size for me. The entire cell was only just a little bigger than the club tree fort back home and was made from large stones with no windows.

"Please sit down, I can tell you had a very long day my little friend," Fat Albert said to me.

I sat down in the chair, "Thanks, it has been a long day! Tell me how you know my name? Why is everyone looking that way at me?" I asked Fat Albert.

"Sure, we have a few minutes before you leave," Fat Albert answered.

"What, I am going somewhere? That Witches wheel gave me 25 years in here," I told Fat Albert.

"I know that, we rigged the wheel, so you would get sent here," Fat Albert explained.

"Thanks, "I said cautiously.

"Well, the pointer could have landed on 'make me a pie," Fat Albert said in response.

I looked at him, "Thanks!"

"You are welcome, now before I tell you our plan, tell me why the Witch is having a party?" Fat Albert asked.

I looked at him and in a sad tone told him, "She murdered the Good Witch of the South just a short time ago."

"What! Ruby, the Good Witch is dead!" cried Fat Albert. Ruby's death was soon being told throughout all the cells and soon every prisoner started to shout.

"RELEASE US!" Every prisoner knew of the Good Witch of the South and loved her very much, now all they wanted was to get their hands on the Evil Witch. The Witch's party was going on, the band was playing music so loud that no one heard the sounds coming from the dungeon's cells below. The Witch was drinking some witches brew out of her favorite mug, enjoying the band, having a wonderful time while she waited for her wicked sister to join her. The Witch invited many guests, like vampires, Wolfman, and many more evil creatures.

Fat Albert started to explain the plan that he was told through the dungeons, "Someday a brave hero will enter and help us out of here, kill both evil witches, which was the last part of the plan."

I did not know what to say after hearing the story, I just thought about it and finally asked, "How can I get out to help?" Fat Albert stood up and pulled the bunk bed away from the stone wall; he then grabbed a hold of a large stone and pulled it out enough for me to squeeze by.

Fat Albert looked at me, "We only have about ten minutes before the guards make the next bed checks; you need to climb up to the next level it will open into a small closet, once inside you will be contacted, now go my friend."

I reached out my hand and thanked Fat Albert, we shook hands, and I started climbing the small size tunnel that Fat Albert had been digging upwards for many years as he was told to do one night long ago in a dream by a talking parrot. I was just the right size for the small tunnel. Fat Albert lit his only fire stick which he had been saving and held it, so I could see where I was climbing. It only took a little while until I felt a flat sided stone. "I've reached the top," I said to Fat Albert.

"Okay, now just slide that flat stone over and climb out, good luck!" Fat Albert responded.

"Thanks Fat Albert," I replied. I slowly slid the flat stone and climbed up and out of the tunnel and slid the stone back.

Fat Albert blew out the fire stick and pushed back the large stone, and then pushed back the bunk beds and thought to himself, "Well, if everything goes right, it won't be long until we crash the Witches party."

I was now inside a closet, I slowly peeped out and looked outside to the cell across the hall.

"Hello Jerry, it is nice to see you, I am Frank," the figure said to me.

"Hello, nice to meet you too," I answered.

"Okay, this is the plan, down the hallway is the control room for every cell in this dungeon, inside there are many buttons that open each cell door on all seven levels, once we get those two guards out of there, you run in and start pushing every button you can, but start on level six, that is this one." The figure stated and asked, "You got that?"

I smiled, "I am ready when you are."

Frank used his water cup and tapped three times on the cell bars, a voice cried from the last cell down the long hallway, "Guard I need you!" The two guards heard the shouting in the control room.

"I wonder what they are shouting about this time?" The guard said to the other one seated next to him.

"Guards get your lazy butts out of those chairs and come see this," the voice said.

"Let's go shut him up," said one of the guards.

"I am going to hit him so hard his mama is going to feel it," the other guard remarked. The two guards opened the locked door and started walking down the hallway swinging their wooden clubs, leaving the control room open and unlocked.

"Okay, get ready," Frank whispered to me. Once the two guards reached the cell making all the noise, a water cup hit the bars letting

Frank know that it was time. "Now, Jerry go for it." I opened the closet door and started to run for the open door at the control room.

.

"What is the matter in here?" The guard asked as he hit the bars of the cell.

"My roommate and I had a bet," the voice said.

The two guards looked at each other and both said, "So what, what has that got to do with us?"

The prisoner answered, "I bet him that you guys are so dumb, that you would both leave the control room and leave the door open." The two guards looked at each other with a puzzled look until they heard a voice saying. "RUN! JERRY RUN!"

They both quickly turned and saw me running towards the control room, "STOP!" They shouted and started running back to the control room. The race was on, but I had a good lead and thinking about Ruby made me run faster than I have ever done before. I reached the open door and entered the control room quickly slamming it closed. In front of me was a large table with dozens of buttons built inside of it with one large speaker box and two chairs in front of it. I walked over and sat down and looked at all the buttons. The two guards tried to open the door, but it was locked.

"Where are the keys?" The guard asked the guard standing next to him.

"I don't have them!" The guard responded. They both looked inside the glass window and saw me smiling at them holding a set of keys.

CHAPTER 16

THERE'S NO PLACE LIKE HOME

"STOP!! DO NOT PUSH those buttons!" The guards shouted at me. I looked down and saw number six and a line of buttons beside it. I started pushing in as many buttons as I could. "OH NO! The guards yelled as they saw the cell doors opening, setting free dozens of mad prisoners. One guard reached the alarm bell and pulled down on the string attached to it, that was the last thing he ever did. Both guards were quickly killed by dozens of prisoners. The alarm bell sounded throughout the castle, I heard it and started pushing buttons on every level until I heard a knock on the door.

"Hey Jerry, open up the door, it's Frank!" Frank said through the door. I stopped and opened the door. "Great job!!" Frank said shaking my hand. "Now, you must escape while we have a dungeon riot." Two prisoners came into the control room and sat down in the chairs and began pushing buttons, opening more cell doors. "Come with me," Frank said. I followed him out into the hallway, prisoners were running for the stairways, they knew about the party on the rooftop and wanted to crash it.

A figure walked over to Frank and me, "Hi guy's, my name is Kyle, and I am going to take Jerry back home to Munchkin Land."

Jerry looked at him, he was a young unicorn, "Glad you made it Kyle, you are just in time," remarked Frank, "Now Jerry get on him and I will help you guys up the stairway onto the rooftop." Kyle knelt, and I climbed on his back. Frank took the ropes that were tied to Kyle's neck and led them both to the stairway that went to the rooftop.

The Witch stood up from her chair, "STOP THE MUSIC!!" She ordered. The band stopped playing and the party guests along with hundreds of flying monkeys listened to the alarm bell going off. "Why is my dungeon alarm bell going off," She screeched. One of the stairway doors opened and a dungeon guard came running out and straight to where the Witch was standing.

"Master, there has been a dungeon break, all the prisoners are being released by that Munchkin boy Jerry!" the guard told the Witch.

"WHAT! That boy has only been in that cell for less than an hour and he broke out and set free all those good people that has taken me hundreds of years to collect." The Witch responded angrily.

"YES, HE DID!!! Soon, he and all those good people, who are now mad, will be coming out of all the stairways headed here," the guard answered.

"I knew I should have made a Munchkin pie out of him. When I catch him, he is going in my oven for sure!" The Witch smirked. The Witch stood on her chair, "It looks like we are going to have some party crashers in a moment, make sure you all give them a warm welcome, but when you see a three-foot little Munchkin, he is all mine!" The flying monkeys and the rest of the Witches party guests did not have long to wait, all four stairway doors from the dungeons opened, out came hundreds of free prisoners running and shouting to repay the Witch and those flying monkeys of hers. In minutes dozens and dozens of hand-to-hand fighting had begun on top of the castle rooftop. The Witch was soon busy aiming her wand at free prisoners, after she hit them, they turned into a small bug that was soon stepped on by hundreds of feet everywhere.

Frank stepped out of the stairway, still holding on to Kyle's ropes, he pulled him out and headed for the nearest castle wall, so Kyle could open his wings and fly off to safety with Jerry. They were there when the Witch spotted them trying to sneak away, "Oh, you guys are not going anywhere," the Witch said.

"I think the Witch has seen us," Frank said as he looked at her across the dozens of fights at the platform where the Witch was now pointing her wand toward them. Kyle and I looked back at the Witch; a lightning bolt came out from the tip of her wand towards Kyle. Frank quickly stood in front of Kyle and took the lightning bolt to his back; he turned into a frog.

I looked at him, and said "Kyle, get us out of here fast or we will be joining him next." Kyle seen the castle wall, it was only a short distance away, he started to run for it, a few flying monkeys tried to stop him, but he raised his two front legs and knocked both out in one kick.

"WOW! Nice kick," I remarked smiling.

"Thanks, my father showed me that one," Kyle replied smiling proudly.

The Witch aimed her wand again, "I won't miss twice." A flying chipmunk grabbed her magic wand out of her hand and flew off towards Kyle and I, we were now standing on the edge of the castle wall.

"Hey, give that back," the Witch said to the flying chipmunk.

The chipmunk looked at her sticking his tongue out, he then turned towards Kyle and I, "Here, take this!" He threw the magic wand at me and flew off to return to the battle below.

I caught the wand and smiled as I looked at it, "I got it!"

The Witch saw me with her wand and yelled, "STOP! GIVE ME BACK MY MAGIC WAND!!!"

I laughed showing off her magic wand to her, and said, "I think this would make a nice present for the Good Witch of the North."

"NO! You cannot do that," she shouted back at him.

"Just try to stop me you old ugly witch," I said back to the Witch. I then whispered to Kyle, "You think I made her mad?"

Kyle laughed, "Yes, my new friend, she is mad."

"Good! Then let us fly back to Munchkin land as fast as you can! I replied with a smile.

"Okay, hold on," Kyle responded laughing. He opened his wings and jumped off the castle wall.

"WOW! This feels great," Kyle said as he flew into the morning rays of the sun just starting to come up.

The Witch saw them fly off, "I'll get you if it's the last thing I ever do!" She then walked over to her broom and picked it up.

"Where are you going master?" A flying monkey asked.

"I will be back, do not worry. My sister will be here shortly, she can manage things here," the Witch replied, then she told her broom, "Broom, follow that unicorn and Munchkin boy and don't lose them." The broom took off and soon was in the air in pursuit.

"So, Kyle, how long has it been since you flew last?" I asked.

"Well, it was right before a dozen flying monkeys caught me about twenty years ago," Kyle explained.

"So, how does it feel to be flying again," I inquired.

"Great! That Witch made me live in a cell too small for me to open my wings all the way up," grimaced Kyle.

"WOW! You sure are a great flyer, we are really moving fast," I said to Kyle.

"I can fly faster than that Witches broom don't worry about that my friend," Kyle proudly remarked. He then looked at the sun rising, "Let me be the first one to say, HAPPY BIRTHDAY!"

"Thanks, Kyle, for the birthday wish and giving me a ride back home," I said in response.

"Oh no, thank you for freeing me and the rest of the prisoners," Kyle said thankfully.

I looked down, "Look, it is the yellow brick road, follow it to Munchkin land."

"Okay with me," Kyle lowered his wings and flew closer to the ground going faster than before, shortly I could see the wall that circled the town of Munchkin.

There it is, my hometown," I said happily. Kyle now flew up to the front gates and landed in front of them. The guard on duty saw it was me and yelled, "OPEN THE GATE, IT'S JERRY AND A FRIEND." The gates opened, Sammy and Ray-Ray came running to meet them.

I jumped off Kyle and met my two best friends, hugging and laughing, Sammy and Ray-Ray shouted, "You did it, the Witch is dead!!"

Soon a crowd surrounded me and picked me up, "Take him to the center of town, the mayor wants to see him," spoke the General of the Munchkin army. I tried to speak up and tell them that the Witch is not dead, but I could not. It did not take long until they carried me to the center of town, and I was set before the Mayor of Munchkin land.

"Well, my boy, your two friends told me about the plan, about how your club of boys were going to kill the Witch of the East." The mayor said, "I couldn't believe it when they, and the Good Witch of the North told me, but it worked, and you killed the Witch of the East." Happily, spoke the mayor.

"NO! I did not kill the Witch, Mayor. I am sorry, but our plan is not finished." I said to the mayor.

The mayor did not get a chance to ask me another question, the alarm bell sounded from the watch tower, the Mayor looked up into the sky and saw the Witch flying on her broom heading our way.

I looked at the mayor and said, "Order everyone back inside their homes, I will take care of her."

The mayor shook my hand and said, "Good Luck my friend. Everyone back to your homes until the danger is gone!" Sammy and Ray-Ray did not go anywhere, they stayed next to me.

"Guys, please go hide in that haystack over there, stay inside, I will be there in a minute after I talk to the Witch. Please do not argue with me on this one." They shook my hand and quickly ran and dove into the haystack.

I looked at Kyle, "Please go back to your home, I need to see the Witch alone."

"I understand," Kyle said. Saying goodbye and ran jumping into the air flying off.

The Witch of the East landed near me and said, "There you are! Now give me back my magic wand or I will destroy this town with my own two hands."

"You mean this wand?" I said as I pulled out her magic wand from behind my back.

The Witch looked at her wand, "YES! That one, now walk over to me and hand it over."

"Okay, but before I do, I want to share my birthday gift that the Good Witch of the South gave to me, with you." I said.

"Oh really? What did my dear departed friend give you on this birthday?" The Witch asked sarcastically.

"A birthday wish, good for one free wish," I said smiling. The Witch looked at me and for the first time in her life she became scared. "I wish that a house will fall from the sky now and land on the pointed black hat of yours leaving only Ruby shoes!!" I then threw her wand back to her and ran fast, jumping into the haystack with Sammy and Ray-Ray, "Well boys, our plan is about to happen! Keep your eyes on the sky."

High above the Witch heard a dark cloud formed in the clear blue sky, the Witch looked up and said, "I better get out of here, I got a bad feeling." She picked up her magic wand from the ground and sat on her broom yelling, "LET'S GET OUT OF HERE!" The broom for the first time did not obey her, it did nothing. She started to panic and pointed her wand at the dark cloud, getting bigger, her magic wand was not working, she then tried to move but her feet were stuck to the ground. "What did you do to me Jerry!" She shouted. The Witch of the East looked up one more time at the sky, and out of the dark cloud a tornado came out. Inside the tornado was someone's house and it was coming straight at her. The Evil Witch screamed as the house fell from the tornado and landed on her, killing her instantly, the pair of Ruby shoes were the only things left of the Evil Witch of the East.

Seventy-five years later, back in real time, King Jerry stopped telling his story. The future King Mikey walked over to him and said, "Thank you King for sharing your first adventure with us, it was a great tale."

"Thank you, now that my story is finished, it is time for me to go," said King Jerry as he stood up and told Mikey to sit in his chair. After Mikey sat down, King Jerry took off his crown and placed it on Mikey's head saying, "Long live our new King of Munchkin land and his future Queen, Zee!" The Good Witch of the North pointed her magic wand into the sky, fireworks started going off high in the sky. All was peaceful in the land of Munchkin again. No Evil Witches or Warlocks!

The end!

www.ingramcontent.com/pod-product-compliance
Lightning Source LLC
Chambersburg PA
CBHW030356180626
46812CB00007B/2902